ALIVE AND ALONE

by W.R. Benton

LOOSE CANNON ENTERPRISES
Petaluma, CA

www.dancingfoxpublishing.com
© Copyright 2013 by W.R. Benton
Cover layout and Design © 2013 Dancing Fox Publishing
Cover art © 2013 by K. O. Haberstroh, used with permission
Edited by: Bobbie La Cour

2014 Edition
Print ISBN 978-1-939812-39-1

Books by W.R. Benton

Western Fiction
Red Runs the Plains
War Paint
James McKay, U.S. Army Scout
The Fur Seekers
Nate Grisham: Black Mountain Man
Jake Masters, Bounty Hunter

Other Books by Gary L. Benton
Simple Survival, a Family Outdoors Guide
Impending Disasters
Bubba's Dawg Might be a Redneck

More info at www.wrbenton.net

Dedication

To Timothy "Timman" Kralik, of Creston, Iowa. Tim's the man!

To all members of our military rescue forces both past and present. As a veteran, I salute you; as a prior life support supervisor, I know your sacrifices are great.

To wife Melanie, where would I be without your understanding?

The renowned artist,
K. O. Haberstroh
created the cover art for this book.

See more of her fine work at:
http://www.westernartandpoetry.com/
She may be contacted by email at:
info@westernartandpoetry.com

Author's Note

For the sake of simplicity and ease of reading, I have changed most dialogs between aircraft, the command post, rescue personnel and Rescue Center. The military uses many acronyms that would make reading difficult, or at least slow it down, for the average civilian. All military ranks are capitalized, out of respect for our military.

While this is a work of fiction, the events very well could happen and in the way I have written them. The United States Air Force is totally dedicated to rescuing both military and civilian personnel in times of need, but there is a limit to all things. Few rescues are called off, unless there is some indicator survival is impossible, but even then, the dedicated crews want to continue. Imagine if you can, training constantly to save a life, and then one day you're finally called to do the job! Of course, not all rescues have a happy conclusion and people die, but thanks to our search and rescue forces, each year many lives are saved that otherwise would be lost.

Our military forces, and not just our rescue teams, are the best-trained men and women in the world today. Why are they so well trained? I had an old Sergeant say to me once, "We train hard in peace so we bleed less in war." I don't think he thought of that as a profound statement, but I do. Our Soldiers, Marines, Sailors, Coast Guard, and Airmen, train hard, and they train to win. However, this book is about search and rescue, who are in my opinion some of the best of the best.

"*That Others May Live*" is the motto of our P.J.'s and it's a good one.

W.R. Benton
Pearl, Mississippi
15 March 2013

CHAPTER 1

The arctic wind was cold in David's face, but his hands shook more from fear than from the cold, as he forced the damaged door open on the small airplane. He could clearly see his father, and while the man did not seem any worse, he looked no better. Blood had dried on his dad's face from a severe cut to his forehead, which had occurred when the airplane crashed onto the side of the mountain. David was scared, not only for his father, but for his own life as well.

"Da. . .Dad? Are you ok?" David asked, his voice filled with fear as he peered into the dark interior of the aircraft wreckage.

A few long seconds passed before the young boy heard his father say in a weak voice, "Son, I'm. . . in bad shape. I . . . don't think . . . I'll make it Dave."

David Wade felt the tears forming in his eyes and he fought back the urge to cry. He was old enough to know he had to keep his wits about him or the two of them were going to die.

"Dad, help will be here soon. I heard you send a Mayday just before we struck the mountain."

David's father gave a loud groan and turned his head slightly so he could make eye contact with his fifteen year old son as he said, "David. . . I don't. . . know if the call was heard by. . . anyone."

How can we survive in this cold and snow? The weather is getting really cold, David thought as he moved inside the small plane to get out of the cutting edge of the knife like wind.

"Find. . . surviv. . . survival kit." His father spoke once again and the voice sounded weaker.

"I have the kit outside near some rocks, but far enough from the plane I can have a fire. I only came back here to help you get out. I tried right after the crash, but your legs are caught in some aluminum sheeting or something. You have to stay strong, dad. We'll survive, and this time next year we'll both be laughing about this."

"David. . . I want you to make. . . a shelter for you. . . yourself. Tonight it will get twenty . . . below maybe."

"What about you? I can't just leave you, dad." David spoke, as he felt his eyes sting from tears that were flowing down his wind burned cheeks, and then added, "Don't make me leave you dad, please."

"So. . . Son, I have internal injuries. You . . . seem to forget, I'm a . . . doctor."

"Tell me what to do to make you better, dad!" David suddenly blurted out.

His father, though in deep pain, gave a weak grin and replied, "Dave. . . I'm not going. . . to live. . . nothing you can do. But, son, promise. . . me, promise me, that. . . you'll try to survive."

David lowered his head, and thought of his mother and his sister back in Anchorage. He knew he could fix his dad up, if he would only tell him what to do. However, the young boy didn't think he could get his father from the aircraft without help, because his legs were mangled in the wreckage. *How can I go home without my dad?* David thought as he raised his eyes and made eye contact with his father.

"Shelter, David. . . fire. . .get out of wind." His father spoke through clenched teeth, as the pain in his stomach grew larger.

"What about you?"

"David! Lis. . . listen to me. I'm a dead. . . man! Son, save yourself. . . now."

David picked up the casualty blanket he'd brought from the first aid kit, wrapped it around his father's shoulders, and then tucked it in at the floor. The blanket appeared to Dave as being made from a lightweight metallic material, but he wasn't sure. It was dark green on one side and shiny silver on the other. He made sure the shiny side of the blanket was toward his father, so his body heat would reflect back at him. He didn't want to leave his father, but he knew that the airplane would get too cold during the night, and the temperature was already dropping. The young boy leaned over and gently kissed the top of his father's head as he fought an almost uncontrollable urge to cry.

"Dad, I'm going now to fix a shelter, but I'll be back in less than an hour. I'll get a shelter up, a fire going, and maybe fix us both some instant soup from the survival kit."

"Good. . . boy. Don't let. . . your mother. . . down. Survive. . . David. I love. . . you." His father spoke, but his voice got lower and lower as he grew tired from the simple task of just speaking.

David turned, wiped the tears from his eyes and cheeks, glanced back at his father, and quickly said as he opened the door to leave, "I'll be back soon, dad, and with a hot drink for you too."

The wind struck him with much more force than it had just a few minutes earlier when he'd gone into the airplane to check on his father. Looking up at the sky, David noticed the clouds were darker, and the sun was sitting in the west. He knew he would only have about

3

five hours of daylight every day now, so he had to use his time wisely or he'd end up dead.

David's right leg hurt, and while it had a long deep scratch on it, the bleeding had stopped a little over an hour ago. His whole body was stiff and sore from the impact of the small plane onto the side of the mountain. *It's a good thing dad is such a good pilot, or we'd both be dead right now,* the young man thought, as he made his way to a group of rocks about a hundred feet from the crash site. David didn't realize his father had pulled the nose of the aircraft up at the last second to allow the force of the impact to be evenly distributed throughout the aircraft frame, reducing the force of impact for the occupants.

Opening the bag marked shelter, David was surprised to find a large piece of tarp, some parachute cord, and some small metal tent pegs. The young man understood a few minutes later that he would have to use the tarp to make a tent. He'd done it many times with his mother's blankets in the back yard, so this should be no harder. Lying under the shelter bag, at the bottom of the survival kit, he discovered a sleeping bag and a wool blanket, but he knew his first task was to get a shelter up, and then he'd worry about comfort. He placed the items aside for the time being, as he stood on tired legs, and then pulled his hunting knife from his sheath.

David had been born and raised in Alaska, which gave him an advantage that he didn't even consider. All of his life, as far back as he could remember, he'd been camping, fishing, hiking, and hunting. His serious hunting had actually just started the year before, but he'd downed a nice caribou and, later in the same season, he'd been able to get a moose. For years he'd gone on hunting trips to help around the campsite as the older boys and men hunted. His father had been responsible for teaching David how to live with nature, and how to live in the wilderness in comfort.

⸙ Doctor James W. Wade had spent four years in the United States Air Force as a survival instructor, and after his discharge, he'd used the educational benefits from his military service to go to college and then on to medical school. He'd done well in Anchorage, and his practice was large. Since he'd left the service while stationed at Elmendorf Air Force Base near Anchorage, James had stayed in the area because he'd fallen in love with not only the beautiful country, but David's mother as well. That had all happened many years past, and during that time, James had added both David and Marie to the family, become qualified as a private pilot, and spent as much time in the bush as he could.

David pulled the hood up on his jacket, and moved into the nearby trees to find some long green limbs. *We're lucky we crashed here, and not above the tree line up north. At least we have trees and some shelter from the wind,* the young man thought as he cut six long green poles, and pulled them back to the protection of the rocks. Once in the rocks and out of the wind, he trimmed the poles carefully to keep the small limbs from puncturing his tarp once placed over the wooden frame.

Dave, you're pretty stupid! He suddenly thought as he felt a deep shiver go through his whole body, *you need a fire and now.* He removed the lighter and fire-starting materials from the bag marked "fire". He noticed he also had two boxes of windproof matches, flint and steel, and a magnesium match. He removed the flint and steel from the container, and placed it in his inside jacket pocket.

5

Since David had selected a shelter out of the wind in the trees, and behind some large boulders, his fire was easy to start and in a matter of a few short minutes, he had a small fire burning. His father had always warned him to keep his fires small, because they used less wood, and for safety purposes to never leave it unattended for very long. Dave kept his fire very small, not much bigger than a dinner plate, and as the damp wood snapped and popped, he walked around his campsite picking up fuel to burn later. He'd indeed been very lucky where they'd crashed the plane; dead wood was all around him.

As soon as he'd gathered enough wood for the fire to burn all night, he laid the green poles over three large boulders, and then draped his tarp over the wooden frame. With the rocks pretty much covering the sides and his tarp on top, David felt his shelter would do for the time being. He quickly tied the parachute cord to the metal grommets in the tarp and tied the cord to the tent pegs. Then, he used a rock to hammer the pegs into the hard half-frozen ground.

Well, it's crude, dude, but it should hold, Dave thought as he pulled on the tarp to see if it was secured. He knew if the weather turned nasty and it started to snow, he would cover the tarp with boughs from the evergreen trees, and then plaster it all with snow. He and his father had once camped during a bad blizzard in a snow-covered shelter just like this and had been warm with only a candle burning inside.

With his shelter up and his fire burning, David opened the pouch labeled food and shook his head in disbelief. He had expected much more, but he knew a person actually needed little food to survive on, as long as they had water. In the bag, he found two dehydrated meals, four chocolate candy bars, and a small bag of hard candy, four containers of dried soup, and four high-energy bars. It was then he remembered his father saying that most rescues happened well within forty-eight hours, so a lot of food was not needed. *I hope you were right, Dad,* Dave thought as he pulled out a metal canteen cup and added the last of his bottled water to the container. He placed the cup near the fire and gazed into the dancing flames as he waited for the water to heat.

As soon as the water started dancing in the cup, David added the dried soup base and stirred it with a plastic spoon from his emergency rations. While he was hungry and scared, he knew his father needed the heat and energy the soup would give him more than he did, so David stood and made his way toward the aircraft wreckage with the metal cup in his right hand.

The young man pulled the door open and didn't notice the loud groan it gave in protest at being moved. It was darker now, almost dusk, and it was hard for him to see inside the aircraft.

"Dad, are you alright?" David asked, as he moved awkwardly into the wreckage to avoid sharp pieces of jagged metal.

Long seconds passed before he heard his father say, "Dave. . . not long. . . now."

David moved to his father's side, and still holding the hot cup in his right hand, he used his left hand to raise his fathers head from his shoulders. "Dad, try to drink some of this, it's hot."

"No. . .Dave, I. . . cannot drink. . . with inter. . . nal injuries. You . . . drink."

David suddenly remembered the small flashlight he had in the pouch behind his father's seat. The pouch also had some candy and another bottle of water. Dave moved his body to the left and using his right hand pulled the flashlight out. Sliding the switch on, the light was bright in the small confines of the wreckage.

Moving the light toward his father's face, the look in his eyes shocked David. His face was deathly pale, and his forehead beaded in sweat. Dried blood covered almost every inch of his dad's face and neck. Fear grew like an over inflated balloon in the young boys mind as he looked into the eyes of a man he both loved and respected. David knew instantly when their eyes met, his father was dying.

"Dad, you hang tough man. Someone will be here soon, you'll see!" The young man suddenly blurted out, his mind about to snap.

"I . . . am tryin', son. I . . . hurt Dave." As his dad spoke, David saw his father's eyes lose focus and then abruptly roll back in his head.

"Dad, don't you die on me!" He screamed as panic filled his very soul.

His father's eyes opened once more and he placed his right hand on David's left arm, which was still holding his head erect, and said, "Dave. . . I . . .love. . .you."

David was watching intently as his father's eyes rolled back once more; a shudder through his entire body, and Doctor James Wade died. It was many minutes later before the young man realized what had happened.

"Dad! Dad! Don't leave me alone, Dad!" He screamed and then in almost a whisper a few seconds later, he pleaded, "Come back Dad! I love you dad, please, don't leave me, Dad!"

Later, David was not sure how long he'd stayed in the wreckage crying. He knew the death of his father had almost killed him, because the inside of the aircraft had grown very cold. He was shaking severely from the start of hypothermia when he once more made his way back to the warmth of his shelter and fire.

Tears froze on his cheeks and his hands no longer had much feeling left in them as he added wood to his dying fire. As the flames ate at the dried wood, the young boy stared into the fire and thought, *What can I do now? How can I tell Mom and Marie that dad is dead? Dad, I love you. Oh, dad, I wish I could have done something to help you.* It was hours later before his head drooped from fatigue, that David Wade entered the void of deep sleep.

CHAPTER 2

O ff and on during the cold and windy night, David added wood to his small fire, though come morning he would not remember doing it. The snow he had expected did not come, but it was about as uncomfortable and cold as the boy could take. He awoke cold, hungry, and aching all over. He knew he should have lined his shelter floor with pine boughs, crawled into his sleeping bag, and gone to sleep, but his mind just didn't seem to function like it normally did. For once in his life, David Wade was alone in the world and the reality of his situation scared him, more than just a little. Even the wind whistling through the trees and rocks seemed to whisper of his coming death.

As he added a couple of small pieces of wood to his fire, David understood he was giving up, and without a fight. *I can't let Dad down, or my mom, he thought as he watched the flames, I have to try hard to survive. I know enough; after all, it should be almost any time now that a rescue team starts looking for us. I have to survive for dad. I know he was worried about me and I have to live for him. What was it dad called the desire to survive? I remember now, he called it the will to survive.*

David pulled the survival kit closer, and started going through all of the items in the kit again, but paying much more attention this time. He found all sorts of things, and some he figured he'd never use. He discovered a plastic whistle, two cans of water, a strobe light, a signal mirror, an Air Force survival manual, a first aid kit, a pocketknife with two blades, a pair of wool gloves, and some other smaller items. He also found a fanny pack with a belt and plastic quick-disconnect buckle, so he could wear it around his waist. He placed some of the signaling gear, the compass, the fire starting equipment, and the two pouches of food in the fanny pack. The rest of the gear he placed inside the plastic survival kit container and then put it inside his shelter.

It was just as he returned to the fire that he remembered the rifles and suitcases they had in the aircraft. He stood and made his way to the wreckage, feeling the pain of his father's death growing as he neared the small plane. He had covered his father's head with the casualty blanket before he'd left him, so at least he did not have to look at his face. He knew if he saw his father, he'd break down again, and right now he could not afford to do that. There was a small storage compartment on the left side of the aircraft, near the tail, that held the suitcases and rifles, so Dave approached the latched door of the compartment. It appeared to be intact and it opened easily once he pushed the latch.

He reached inside and pulled out two small overnight bags, and then removed two rifles in protective plastic containers. Finally, reaching to the very rear of the compartment, he pulled out a small military ammunition can that held the shells for both rifles. David knew there were fifty bullets for each gun stored in the can, and for the first time since the crash, he felt some relief. He'd grown up hearing stories of killer grizzly bears and wild attacking moose, so having a weapon at least made him feel more secure and safe.

David picked up the equipment and made his way toward camp as quickly as his stiffened body would allow. The wind, though still blowing, had much less of a bite than the day before. *Temperature has gone up a little,* he thought, as he neared his fire.

Kneeling beside the small blaze, he placed the metal canteen cup near the flames and added a cup of water. As the water heated, he opened the overnight bags and sorted the clothing into piles, which he placed inside the shelter. He kept out a sweater, wool socks, and his hiking boots. He then opened the plastic gun carriers, and checked both of the guns very closely. His father's rifle had a cracked stock and the scope was hanging loose from the mounting rings. David placed the damaged rifle inside the shelter, and then pulled his own rifle from the protective plastic case.

His rifle was still in good condition, but he knew the scope was likely out of alignment from the hard impact of the crash. He was not concerned, and using his pocketknife, he removed the scope and placed it in his coat. He'd use the scope as a monocular now. He could hit pie plates at a hundred yards using the open sights on his rifle, so he was sure he'd survive with his own gun along. The sling and mounts were still secured, so he'd not have to carry the rifle in his hands all the time. Both of the guns were of the same caliber, 30.06, so he knew it would drop big game if needed, but more importantly, he now had a hundred rounds of ammunition for his rifle.

By mid morning, the snow finally started to fall, and the flakes were the big lazy kind that took forever to reach the ground. David had always loved falling snow, and had spent his youth learning to ski, operating a snowmobile, and ice-skating. While he was at home in the bush, he had never in his life felt so alone and scared as he did at this moment.

13

The lack of noise is so loud, he thought, as he cut pine boughs to place on top of his shelter, *and I'll bet a lot of people would not be able to stand the quiet.*

He then remembered his father warning him of what most people experienced when faced with a survival situation, "David, the key to staying sane in a survival situation is to stay busy. Keep firewood gathered, look for edible plants, find water sources, make your shelter better, and set snares out to trap small game. Also, keep your clothing in good repair and stay as clean as you can under the circumstances. If you don't stay busy and active, your mind will start to feel pity about the situation you're in, and that will make it harder for you to survive."

David went back to the aircraft, and went through the pouches behind the seats, checked the floor and dash, looking for anything of value. He found little, but he did cover his Dad's body better, and felt more comfortable as he did so. Dave knew his father was dead beyond any doubt, and while he felt a horrible pain each time he looked at his body, he understood his father would want him to survive. To survive meant he'd have to take anything he needed from the aircraft, and use it to help keep him alive. Nonetheless, tears stained his cheeks as he walked back toward the fire.

Once at the crude shelter, David placed the few items he'd found in the aircraft near the fire. He'd found a book he'd been reading, a couple of old magazines, two candy bars, and pair of sunglasses. *Not much here,* he thought as he sat by the flames, pulled his legs up, and wrapped his arms around them.

Suddenly David felt very sad, and recognized quickly that he had to get moving or he'd start feeling sorry for himself. He stood, picked up his rifle, and slung it over his right shoulder. Walking to the survival kit, he pulled out a long length of brass snare wire and placed it in his right pants pocket. He had decided to stay busy, so he'd put out a few snares to see if he could catch some wild game to eat. The snow was still falling slowly, and the ground was just barely covered. Dave knew the snow could fall for days like this, and in the end, he could end up with thirty inches or more on the ground. He also knew bad weather would make it more difficult for anyone looking for him to find his location. But, he'd already decided he'd survive, so he was not going to start feeling sorry for himself and give up.

He made a few simple snares by making a locking loop in the wire that would slide up and down smoothly. The survival book had shown illustrations on how to make the loop, and had suggested he place them on game trails. Looking as hard as he might, Dave could find nothing around him that remotely looked like the game trail shown in the book. Finally, out of frustration, he placed them in scattered locations about a hundred yards from his camp.

He had just turned to walk back to his shelter when he saw the smoke. A long dark gray finger of smoke was rising near where his shelter should be. David knew immediately what had happened; he'd left his fire burning unattended for too long! As fast as he could, he ran toward his shelter, and felt his fear mounting as he neared. The last thing in the world he needed was to lose his survival gear and his shelter.

* * *

In Anchorage David's mother picked up the ringing telephone, "Hello, Cathy Wade speaking."

"Cathy, this is Frank." Colonel Frank Wilcox was the commander of the search and rescue squadron at Elmendorf, and a good friend of her and her husband's.

"Frank, any word yet on the plane yet?"

"We now know Jim sent a short mayday or said something to indicate he was having mechanical problems with his aircraft. The message was hard to hear and very difficult to understand. It was sent at about the same time he disappeared from our radar screens. Some of our audio experts here at the base are attempting right now to enhance the volume."

"Do you think they are still alive, Frank?" Cathy had lived in Alaska all of her life, and knew the odds of surviving a mountain crash were remote, but it did happen at times.

There was complete silence on the phone for a second or two; then Frank replied, "Cathy, I don't really know. As you know, a lot depends on how they crashed and where they crashed. But, remember, Jim is a doctor and a good one too. And, don't forget, he used to teach survival in the Air Force, so he has a much better chance than most people would have of surviving. The key to this whole thing is whether or not they survived impact when the plane crashed."

"Frank, Jim knows how to survive, and, I guess, well, I know all of what you just told me. I'm just at a complete loss on what to do now. I'm so scared, Frank."

"Cathy, I'm sending Carol over to spend a few hours with you, because this is not one of those times you should be alone. I'm still at the command post, and tied up with the organization of the search aircraft and crews. I suspect I'll be here all night. The weather has turned nasty where Jim's plane was last on radar, and it's slowing down our rescue efforts. But, Cathy, as soon as I hear anything you'll be the first person to know."

Cathy, feeling tears in her eyes, choked up a little then replied, "Tha. . .thanks Frank. Tell Carol I'll put the tea on."

As she hung up the phone, Cathy Wade dried her eyes with the back of her left hand, and walked to the kitchen counter, where she plugged in her electric teapot. As she reached down and turned it on, she prayed, *Please, God, let both of my men be safe.*

Carol Wilcox lived only a few doors down the street, so it was less than thirty minutes later when Cathy heard the doorbell ring. Wrapping her housecoat around herself a little tighter, she quickly made her way to the door.

"Hello, Cathy, Frank just called and told me the news. I rushed right over; I hope it's okay," Carol spoke with a thick Southern drawl as soon as the door was opened. She'd been raised in Mississippi and sounded it.

"It's fine Carol. I'm just worried sick about my two boys. Come on in, I've the tea on already."

Soon they were both sitting at the kitchen table holding a cup of hot steaming tea. They said nothing as the tea was poured, and each woman added sugar or milk to her cup.

Finally, Carol said, "Look, Cathy, you've got some of the best trained people in the world lookin' for them. Frank told me there are fifty airplanes workin' with the search team and each plane has a qualified spotter. If Jim and Dave have crashed they'll find them, and we both know it."

Cathy lowered her eyes and asked, "But, will they still be alive when they're found?"

Moments of long silence followed but finally Carol replied, "Cathy, I can't answer that, and you know it. If they survived the crash, I know beyond a doubt Jim would be able to survive in the woods. My goodness, he was a fully qualified Air Force survival instructor, and Dave is not far behind him in ability. They are both capable in the woods, so I'd not worry about that

17

part. Right now is the hardest part, because we have to wait and let Frank and his troops do their jobs."

"But, what if they're dead?"

Carol lowered her eyes to her teacup, and then said, "Cathy, I hope they're both alive and doing well, but if they're dead, then they're dead. There won't be a thing we can do to change that, and you know it. I think you're puttin' the cart before the horse here. Let's wait and see what Frank finds as soon as this weather breaks."

"I'm so frightened Carol. I feel so alone." Tears gathered in her eyes, and then slowly made their way down her cheeks.

"You ain't alone Cathy, and you'll never be. I'm here for you, and Frank and his people are committed to findin' your boys for you." Carol spoke as she stood and then walked to Cathy's chair, where she put her hand on the woman's shoulder as she continued, "And if you feel like cryin' Cathy, then have at it. I guess any woman in your shoes right now, would shed more than just a few tears."

Less than an hour later, as the two women sat in the living room watching television, the show was interrupted with a special news broadcast. "The Anchorage office of the FAA announced this afternoon that a small aircraft, piloted by Doctor James Wade of Anchorage, has been missing for more than twelve hours. Elmendorf Air Force Base has search and rescue crews standing by for a break in the weather, but according to Colonel Frank Wilcox, the squadron commander, all activities are on hold until the weather improves. Doctor Wade and his son, David Wade, were flying southwest of Anchorage and disappeared off radar screens late yesterday. We will keep you updated as more information becomes available. This is Rodney J. Calbreath, reporting."

Once again, Cathy broke into tears, and Carol moved closer to her friend and gave her a big hug. It was at that moment Marie opened the front door and walked up the stairs to the living room.

Marie threw her books onto the floor near a big overstuffed chair, looked at her mother and then asked, "What's the matter mom? Has something bad happened?"

Carol, realizing Cathy was in no shape to explain things to the young girl said, "Marie, you father and David are both missin'. Their plane went off the radar screens late yesterday afternoon."

"Are they ok?"

"Honey," Carol was unsure how to answer at first, but then replied, "We don't know yet. My husband, Frank, has crews ready to search for them, but the weather is too bad for them to go out right now."

"When will we know? How could they crash? Dad was a very good pilot!"

"Marie, we just don't know all of that yet. Frank will find them, but it will take time."

The young girl moved to her mother's side, put her right arm around her neck, and pulled her close. Carol felt her heartbreak as mother and daughter both broke into tears of anguish. *Frank, please, do somethin' and quickly! It's the not knowin' that is the hardest part for these kind people,* she thought, as she stood and made her way into the kitchen. The least she could do was make dinner, not that they'd eat, but it was something to do. Besides, Marie and Cathy deserved the time alone to reach to an understanding of what might have happened.

Dinner was quiet and very little eating was done. Finally, Cathy threw her fork onto her plate, stood and began to pace the floor. At that moment, the phone rang.

"Cathy Wade speaking," Cathy spoke into the phone quickly.

"Cathy, this is Frank again. My crews have gone out and started the search. Now, I also have word from my audio fellows, and they tell me Jim did, in fact, transmit a very weak mayday call just before he went off radar. We now have a pretty good idea where the plane went down, so all we can to do is pray this weather will hold until we can find the site."

"Frank, it's dark out. How can they find the plane in the dark?"

"Each aircraft, by Federal law, has an emergency locator beacon in the tail. When the aircraft crashes, the beacon starts to transmit on guard, or what you would call our emergency frequency. It doesn't have the range to transmit far, but if one of my planes gets near the crash site the beacon will still be transmitting." Frank attempted to sound excited, but he knew that severe cold weather could affect the transmitter's battery life, so the battery could already be dead. Or, worse yet, the transmitter could have been damaged on impact. Only he didn't say any of these things. Since he'd been in the rescue business a long time, he wanted to give Cathy some hope, and yet remain honest with her, because right now hope was all she had.

"Would your spotters be able to see a fire on the ground?"

"It depends on the cloud cover, but it's possible. Right now, I want you to let me talk to Carol, and then I want you and Marie to come over to my house for the night. That way you won't be alone, and the last thing you need is to stay in that house."

CHAPTER 3

By the time the rescue aircraft were in the air, David had the fire out at his campsite, and was taking inventory of the damage done by the flames. He'd lost most of his survival equipment, and his father's rifle was nothing but a hot piece of blackened steel. David knew he'd been lucky, because he'd not made his shelter under a tree, and as a result the fire had simply burned the pine boughs he'd place on top of the shelter, and on the floor of the structure to insulate him from the cold ground. The last thing he needed was a forest fire on his hands. But, at the moment, the young man felt anything but lucky, because he'd lost almost everything he'd gathered up to help him survive.

Dang, almost all I have left is what I had on me or in my fanny pack! I think I can use part of the sleeping bag, but that's about it. How could I have been so dumb! I knew better too! he thought in anger as he dug through the remains of his survival gear. The survival container was now just one large lump of melted plastic. The young man noticed the plastic from the survival kit had run completely over the gear that had been stored inside, and then hardened once the fire was out. Dave considered trying to force the melted plastic open, but he knew anything inside had been damaged to the point it was now useless to him. He shook his head and then threw the lump of hard plastic into the now worthless shelter in frustration.

The snow had continued to fall, but slowly, and very little was on the ground, perhaps less than an inch. David was angered by his carelessness with the fire, but he knew he had to erect another shelter of some sort or he'd freeze to death way before morning. He understood then that the loss of the survival manual was his biggest loss, and while some of it had not burned up, more than half was gone. He'd glanced through the book that morning, and it had a lot of information he needed now, but it was almost completely destroyed, and of little use to him. All that remained of the book was a section on how to gut and eat wild animals, and another on how to find water.

What was it Captain Johnston had said to dad at the picnic that day, about making survival shelters in the snow and cold? If I remember right, he said a large pine tree could be used if a man trimmed the lower branches off. But, I can't have a fire because the tree would go up like a match once it started to burn, David thought as he unconsciously picked up a stick and started dragging it around in the snow at his feet.

Standing, he saw a large pine about fifty feet from where he stood, and it was a nice full one. He still had his sheath knife, so he made his way to the tree, and started removing the lower branches. Some of the branches were dead, so he broke them off and pulled them away from his shelter. The live branches he cut from the tree, and then lined the cold ground with them. As he worked, he thought of how he could stay alive tonight when the temperature went way down.

Finally, he decided he could pull a small piece of aluminum from the aircraft wreckage, and use it to construct a small container for his fire. By burning small twigs, he could have a very small fire near the shelter all night long, and yet not have it actually inside. This time he'd never leave it unattended.

David had learned a few years back how to make a heat reflector using boulders or logs to make the heat from a fire reflect back into a shelter. It was basically a wall on the opposite side of the entrance to a shelter, with the fire in the middle, and it usually worked very well, unless the wind picked up. He had plenty of wood, so he pulled eight large logs to the area he'd selected to make his heat reflector. Using his knife, he peeled the bark from each log, and then pounded four large stakes into the frozen ground, two at each end of where the logs would lay. The stakes were set far enough apart to allow him to stack the logs on top of each other, and the poles would hold the logs upright.

At times, he noticed he was working hard enough to break out in a sweat, so he'd stop and allow himself time to cool down. He knew from cross-country skiing that sweating could be fatal in cold weather. The sweat would freeze, and form a thin layer of ice on a person, which could cause death. *Strange,* he thought as he wiped the sweat from his forehead, *how things I learned in different sports and subjects are coming together to help me.*

As soon as his heat reflector was competed, he went to the aircraft wreckage and pulled a large piece of metal from under the wing. Being careful not to cut his hands on the sharp sheet metal, he made his way back to camp. Once in camp, he placed the end of the metal under a log of his reflector, and pushed down on the soft metal, causing it to bend. He repeated the process on all four sides, and ended up with a very crude looking metal bowl.

Using rocks under the raised lips of the container to stabilize it, he soon had a small fire going in the very center of the metal. This time he used the flint and steel, not his matches to start the fire. He had considered using the matches, only he knew he should save them for real emergencies. David had always loved starting a fire with flint and steel, just like the old time mountain men had done when they were out trapping beavers. He knew the secret to starting a fire was to have your tinder, kindling, and fuel nearby before you ever started to work on it. Of course, his father had always reminded him that all wood used in a fire should be as dry as possible, because it burned faster, and gave off less smoke as it burned. The thought of his father brought tears to his eyes once more.

As he waited for the fire to die down a bit so he could cook something to eat on the hot coals, he opened one of the survival meals his father had placed in the survival kit. The brownish colored plastic container read, MRE and in smaller print, it stated below, Meal Ready to Eat. The ration looked like a military meal to David, and while he'd never eaten one, he'd seen Colonel Wilcox eat them on a hunting trip the year before. If it was the same meal the colonel had eaten, it was not dehydrated, and Dave and his father had always used the commercial dehydrated meals when they camped. They both like them because they were very lightweight and tasted good.

He opened the plastic, pulled the contents out, and placed them in his lap, as he looked the items over closely. He discovered the large bag contained a main entrée, a side dish, crackers, coffee, cream, sugar, salt, pepper, peanut butter, hot sauce, an apple cinnamon energy bar, and a fork/spoon combination. All of the contents were in the same brownish plastic and, as he looked closer, he noticed his entrée was beefsteak. His side dish was mashed potatoes, and David loved steak and mashed potatoes.

The young man had not realized how hungry he was and decided, as his stomach growled in anticipation of the meal, to have the crackers and peanut butter as he heated the meal over his small fire. The directions on the container said the pouches were not plastic, but a type of foil, and he could heat them up in boiling water. He placed his canteen cup, filled with water, on the hot bed of coals from his fire, and then dropped the foil packs containing the meat and potatoes in the water.

The crackers were a little harder than the average soda cracker, but as hungry as he was, they tasted fine. Using his knife, he cut the corner from the peanut butter pouch, and squeezed it out onto the crackers as he ate. He decided to keep the coffee, sugar and cream for breakfast, along with an energy bar. David had never cared much for the taste of coffee, too bitter, but he suspected it would taste just fine in the morning when the temperature was much lower.

He thought back of the movies he'd seen, where hungry men would wolf down their food as quickly as possible. As soon as he'd removed the meat and potatoes from the hot water and opened the pouches, he ate very slowly. For the first time in his short life, Dave did not gulp his food down, but instead he savored each and every bite. Once the pouches were empty, he used his knife to open them up and licked the foil lining clean.

The weather was growing worse, and while the wind had died down, the snow was now falling harder. The temperature was falling as well, and he glanced at his woodpile, hoping he had enough to last the night. He had lined the ground under the tree with pine boughs, so he knew he would sleep off the cold ground, but his sleeping bag was about shot.

He picked up the sleeping bag, and noticed with a critical eye that only about half of the bag remained. He considered his options, and recognized his bag would not protect him over night, and he'd freeze to death if he attempted to use it. His only choice, as he saw it, was to return to the plane, remove the casualty blanket from his father's body, and then cover his head with the partial sleeping bag. He disliked taking the blanket from his father, but knew his dad was beyond being cold any longer, and would want him to use it. Still, the casualty blanket had been his father's death shroud, and it seemed wrong in David's mind to remove it. It took Dave well over an hour to work up enough courage to go back to the plane to retrieve the blanket.

Snow covered the top of the wreckage when David arrived, and he reminded himself to clean it off in the morning. He wasn't sure, but he suspected because of its large size it would be easier to see from the air than a human. He opened the door to the airplane, and slowly made his way to his father's seat. Without turning on the flashlight, he removed the casualty blanket from his father, and it was when he was placing the sleeping bag over his dad's head that his hand came in contact with his father's face. David jerked his hand back as if he had touched a live coal from his fire; the coldness of his father's skin shocked him. He suddenly started crying, and with tears streaming down his face, he placed the remains of the sleeping bag over his dad's head, and then wiped his eyes.

"Dad, I'm so sorry. I don't know if I'll be back dad, because I'm having a hard time visiting you. I love you dad, and you'll always have a place in my heart." Dave spoke aloud, turned, and then crawled from the wreckage. As he closed the door to the plane, the young man knew the wreckage had become a shrine to his father. David understood he would never see an airplane again without thinking of his father, and how he'd died.

It was later that night before the snow stopped, and the temperature dropped a little. He was sitting near the fire to keep warm and sipping on hot water. It was late, but off in the distance he heard the lonely howl of a wolf calling out to another member of its pack. *That has to be the saddest sound in the world,* he thought, just as the last of the wolf's howl trickled off, and the night became silent once more.

David looked at his watch to check the time and saw it was broken. He removed the watch and started to throw it away, then thought better of the idea, and slipped it in his fanny pack. Standing and stretching, the young man suddenly felt very alone once again. He thought about his feelings for a moment and realized the howl of the wolf had triggered his emotions. The wolf had sounded so alone, and the sound reflected how David felt.

He slowly turned, made his way under the large pine tree, and then wrapped up in the casualty blanket. Before he realized he was tired, David had fallen asleep.

Morning dawned cool, but the sun was shining, and the temperature had risen enough that David knew the snow would melt from the ground before noon. He had a quick breakfast of the instant coffee with a sugar and dehydrated cream in the canteen cup. He was in no hurry as he leaned against a large log, and slowly sipped his coffee, enjoying the heat flowing through his body. He was wondering when the rescue teams would find him. While he didn't know much about how search and rescue worked, he knew when they didn't show up in Anchorage, the police would be notified. Well, he thought as he raised the hot cup to his lips, *today will be forty-eight hours. If all goes well, I'll be home this time tomorrow.*

Suddenly he remembered his snares, and quickly finished the bitter tasting coffee as he thought about having fresh meat to eat. While David had shot game, he'd never trapped before, and was unsure what he would do if an animal was caught in one of his snares. Standing, he picked up his rifle, slung it over his right shoulder, and started out to check his traps.

His first two snares were empty, with no tracks in the snow. He moved on through the trees and in the next one, he saw a rabbit caught in the snare. While the survival manual had stated that the snare would choke the trapped animal to death, this rabbit was still very much alive. As David neared the snare the rabbit began to move in an attempt to escape, but the wire held the animal firmly around the neck.

Now what, he thought, as he stood back from the snare, and watched the animal struggle to escape, *I don't want to kill it, but I have to eat.*

Picking up a large stick laying near the trail, David approached the rabbit slowly, and then he struck it as hard as he could on the top of the head. The animal died instantly, and while he was saddened to kill, the young man knew he had no choice if he were to survive. He then reset his snare and move on to the next trap.

The next two traps were empty, but his last one held a small fox by the leg. David was scared to attempt to kill the larger animal with his stick, so he raised his rifle, sighted on the animal's chest, and squeezed the trigger. The fox fell unmoving. The young boy quickly gutted the fox, but left the skin on, and as soon as he was finished, he headed back to camp.

David spent the next hour skinning the fox and cutting meat from the bones. He placed the fox meat in a tee shirt, and using some electrical wires from the plane, he tied it up high in a tree. He'd twisted the wires together to make a crude rope of sorts. He did this so animals could not get at his hard-earned food. The rabbit was placed on a spit, and then over the hot coals of his campfire. He had decided to roast the meat, and it smelled good as he pulled out the burned and scorched remains of the survival manual to see if he could learn anything about cooking or dressing the game better the next time.

On page 108 of the manual, it suggested the inner organs (heart, liver, kidneys) and all meaty parts of the skull—brains, tongue, and eyes be kept as well. David picked up the rabbits head, glanced at it, and then threw it far out into the bush. *I'm not that hungry yet,* he thought, as he fought down the urge to throw-up. But, on another page, it suggested he boil the meat he got, and not roast it. The chapter explained that he'd get more nutrition out of boiled meat than he would if he roasted it. Roasted meat allowed the oils and nutrients to drip onto the fire, where they burned up, and did him no good.

"I'll boil all meat from now on to stay as strong as I can," he spoke aloud as he closed the manual.

As his meat browned over the coals, Dave started remembering Boy Scouting trips when he'd been active with his troop. A few times they had gone on weekend camping trips, and once a scoutmaster had pointed out that pine needles could be used to make tea. They'd tried some, but the tea had tasted bitter to Dave then, but he'd not been attempting to survive at the time either. According to the scout leader, the tea would keep a person from getting scurvy, and anything that would help him stay healthy he wanted.

The young boy spent a good hour gathering up pine needles, but stayed near his camp as his rabbit cooked on the small fire. Not once during the whole time was he ever out of sight of the flames of his fire, because he feared another fire would result in his death. He knew he had to be responsible if he wanted to survive, and return to his mother and sister alive.

David had just sat down and pulled a rear leg from the roasted rabbit when he heard the sound of an aircraft. He quickly placed the cooked meat on the log, and ran to the area of the aircraft wreckage. He screamed, jumped up and down, and waved his arms violently to attract attention. The aircraft passed right overhead, and David knew he'd been seen ...or had he?

The aircraft never changed course, and what concerned Dave was the simple fact that the aircraft did not rock its wings or give any indication he'd been spotted. As the sound of the airplanes engines grew fainter and fainter, and then finally disappeared into clouds off in the distance, he fell to his knees in the mud from the melting snow and cried.

An hour later, as Dave sat by the fire, he realized he'd made no attempt to signal the passing search plane. He knew, from flying with his father, it was difficult to spot things on the ground, even when you knew where they were. He remembered his fanny pack, pulled it around, and started looking at the gear he'd saved from the fire by having it in the pack. He pulled out a signaling mirror, the plastic whistle, and a smoke flare. *Darn it! If I had been prepared, I could have used this smoke flare as the plane came near me! Stupid! Oh, please, let them come back this way. Please, just one more time,* he pleaded as he placed the mirror and whistle around his neck. He stuck the flare in his coat pocket for easy access. He knew he'd just made a horrible mistake, and he hoped it was his last one.

CHAPTER 4

Colonel Frank Wilcox sat at his kitchen table and sipped his hot coffee slowly. It was early morning, his eyes were rimmed in red, and his hands shook from a lack of sleep as he spoke, "We flew right over Jim's last known route, but we saw nothing. While there was still some snow on the ground, most of it had melted."

Cathy, who had been staring into her cup, looked up and met the man's eyes as she asked, "But, what about the ELT you told me about?"

Frank shook his head slowly and replied, "Cathy, I don't know why it isn't sending. I talked to my experts about that, and they said the severe cold we had the last few days might have caused the battery to die, or the transmitter might have been damaged on impact."

"If the airplane hit hard enough to damage the transmitter, wouldn't that much force kill both Jim and Dave?" She asked as her eyes started to water.

"No, maybe not at all. See, the transmitter is located in the tail section of the airplane and it's possible, if Jim nosed up just before impact, that the tail took a lot of the impact forces. The force of that impact might have damaged the ELT." Frank lowered his coffee cup to the saucer, looked at Cathy and then continued, "Cathy, there are too many things that can happen when a plane crashes. What has my rescue teams excited is the fact we did not find any signs of a fire from the crash. Now, there is a good chance a pilot with Jim's experience could land a crippled airplane, so maybe it is almost undamaged. And that, my dear, means they could both be alive."

Cathy's eyes met, his and she could see he had meant exactly what he had just said, they might both still be alive. The woman thought about her husband and son for a minute or two, then asked, "What kind of terrain did the plane go down in, Frank?"

"Mostly mountains, or at least the last known position of the aircraft was in the middle of a mountain range. While the terrain is rough, it is better for survival than the tundra, or in open water. As you might guess, in the water there would be little hope of survival, as cold as the ocean is right now."

"Frank, you need a quick shower, some food, and then to get some sleep." Carol commanded as she walked to the table from the counter where she'd just put on a fresh pot of coffee.

"I will in a minute. Cathy, I left Major Barnes in charge, and he promised to call if they discover anything new during the search. This search will go on now twenty-four hours a day and seven days a week until we either find them, or else the General calls the search off."

Cathy, afraid of the answer asked, "And, Frank, how long do you think the search teams will look for the plane?"

Frank Wilcox shook his tired head, glanced down at his coffee cup, and then said, "I'd guess we'll look for a week to two weeks. Our experience shows if we don't find any sign of them within that time, well, we might never find them. The overall cost of the operation is the deciding factor, Cathy. It is very expensive to run a search and rescue effort, just in aircraft fuel alone."

"What are the chances of the plane being found, Frank? And, I want the truth from you." Cathy asked, dreading the response from the crusty old Air Force Colonel.

"Well," Frank said, then took a quick sip of his coffee before continuing, "pretty good actually, because we find more than we don't find. I'd say the odds are excellent that we'll turn up something. The hardest part right now, and you know this, is the waiting."

Carol, who had not spoken much that morning, suddenly said, "Frank Wilcox, Colonel or not, you get in the shower. And, you, Cathy, need some sleep too. You were up all night, and if you don't go and try to sleep I'm goin' to call Doctor Williams, and have him give you some medications to make you sleep. You're both a couple of very tired people, and we all have to stay strong, not only for Jim and David, but for Marie as well."

Cathy's eyes filled with tears, she slowly nodded in agreement, and then said, "Carol, I just don't know how I can live if I lose both of my men."

Carol, placed her hands on her hips and said, "Carol Wade, right now we don't know that you have lost a blame thing, except maybe an airplane and a lot of sleep. It's like Frank just told you a minute ago, it's the waitin' that is stressful. Now, use the guest bedroom, lie down, and try to sleep. I promise to awaken you the minute I hear somethin'."

Cathy stood and felt a deep fatigue in her whole body. Her eyes felt as if they had sand in them and her legs were tired. As she walked toward the bedroom she thought, *Please God, keep Jim and David safe for me. I love and need them.*

Frank, still sitting at the table, waited until he heard the door to the guest bedroom shut, then said to Carol, "We should have found something already. Ribas flew

33

the same flight path Jim filed, and yet they saw nothing at all. He reported the ground was rough, with mountains and deep gorges, but I can't figure out why the ELT didn't work."

Sitting down beside her tired husband, Carol replied in a tired voice, "Frank, I've heard your search and rescue stories for years. We both know there are strange things that happen at times when a plane goes down. The two most obvious situations are they were both killed on impact, or else one or both of them are attemptin' to survive out in the bush."

"Well, I hope they survived the crash. Jim Wade has the education, training, and experience to survive out in the bush forever, or for at least a very long time. I've been camping with him in the deep snows of the Arctic Circle, way above the tree line, and he did it in comfort, too! The man is an expert at staying alive in situations that would kill a normal person."

Carol took a sip of her tea, gave Frank a worried look and asked, "But, what if Dave is alone? How do you think he'd be able to survive by himself?"

Frank, a man who'd spent over twenty-two years in rescue and recovery, thought for a minute, gave a weak grin and said, "David has been a boy scout, he has done a lot of cross country skiing, and he's grown up in Alaska, so he's got good cold weather smarts. Also, he's been camping, fishing, and going to hunting lodges or on remote hunting trips for years. More than once over the years, I sat by a campfire at night camping with those two, and listened to Jim tell David about how to survive in the bush. But, Cathy, what worries me is the fact most survivors of an airplane crash are usually seriously injured."

"But, Frank, Jim is a doctor."

"What if Jim didn't survive the crash, and Dave is alone and injured on some mountain side? How long do you think a fifteen year old boy can survive out in the Alaskan wilderness if he has been seriously hurt?"

"Can you send in dogs and men to do a ground search?"

Frank shook his head and his eyes showed his frustration as he replied, "Of course we can't at this point, Carol. The flight path is too long and over some of the roughest country in the world. It would take years for men on the ground to cover half the distance, and there is no assurance that in the last few minutes Jim didn't veer off course in an attempt to find a softer place to put his plane down. He could have crashed miles from where he went off of radar."

"I don't understand. Can't you just go to where the plane went off the radar screen and find the airplane?"

The colonel gave a tired chuckle and said, "Carol, baby, I wish it was that simple. See when an airplane drops too low it goes off the radar screen because our radar system cannot tell it from the clutter on the ground. Now, let's say the minimum altitude for a radar system to identify an aircraft is a five hundred feet. Well, a plane in trouble could fly maybe another fifty to a hundred miles, depending on what the problem was aboard the aircraft."

"That far? Ain't it dangerous to fly that low?"

"We did it all the time in Vietnam and Desert Storm. In combat, military pilots often fly below a thousand feet and they do it very fast too, so radar cannot pick them up on their screens. So, as you can see, the search is anything but simple. Only, knowing Jim, I know he'd try his best to find a soft spot to crash on, and he'd also try to stay as close to his original flight plan as possible. The man was not only a very good doctor; he was also a smart pilot."

"What do you think might have happened, Frank? I mean about them survivin' the airplane crash."

35

"Carol, I don't honestly think Jim is alive, or if he is, he's severely injured. If he had made it out of the crash, he would have had signals out for our planes when they flew over this morning. But, we saw nothing at all, and that is not a good sign to me."

Carol gave a low moan, and then asked, "And, what about Dave?"

Frank thought for a moment, and then replied, "He's a smart young kid, and we both know that. I don't think signals would have entered his head, especially if Jim was dead or seriously hurt. Now, one of two things happens to most survivors as soon as they realize they're all alone. They become irrational due to stress and trauma of the situation, or they dust off their pants and start the struggle for survival. I see Dave as the kind that would do both."

"Both?"

"Yep, I think that for the first twenty-four hours, especially if something happened to Jim, Dave would not be thinking clearly, and perhaps he'd be seriously depressed. But, and remember this, the young man has a strong mind and he knows the woods, so eventually he'd bounce back, and start to do what needs to be done."

"I really hope so, Frank. If Cathy loses both Jim and David, she'll have a hard time of it. As a matter of fact, I think tomorrow I'll make appointments for her to see a doctor and to visit the pastor of her church."

Frank lifted his cup, drained the last of the coffee, gave Carol a weak smile, and then said, "I think that is a great idea. The key right now is to keep her physical condition sound, and to keep her emotionally stable as well. Besides, I can assure you, the United States Air Force is not beyond calling on God when the situation calls for it, and right now I feel it does."

"Ok, I'll make the appointments, but right now it's off to the shower for you and, as soon as you're done, get something to eat. I want you in bed and asleep within the hour. You need to stay rested with a clear head Frank, if you're going to help Jim and Dave."

Cathy rolled around in the big bed for hours, and she was unsure if she ever slept or not. Her exhausted mind filled with horror at the prospect of losing half of her family in one day, so what rest she got did not come easy. It was near noon when she got out of bed and showered. She had brought a small overnight bag, so she removed her jeans, underwear, blouse, and quickly dressed. Cathy knew she needed to talk to some people, because she knew her body well, and she could not continue with little sleep and no eating. *I must stay strong for Marie,* she thought as she pulled her socks on.

Upon entering the kitchen, Carol gave Cathy a big friendly smile and said, "Well, you still look tired, but much better. Cathy, I hope I don't upset you, but I made an appointment for you to see your doctor this afternoon, and your pastor this evenin'. Both of them are concerned about you, and worried about Jim and Dave, as well."

Cathy sat down at the kitchen table as Carol walked toward her with a small plate in her right hand, and replied, "No, I did some thinking this morning, before I went to sleep, about the same thing. I haven't slept much the last two nights, because I'm worried sick over waiting. Maybe I can get through all of this with the help of the doctor and my pastor."

Carol placed the plate in front of Cathy and said, "Now, there ain't much on this plate, two eggs, two strips of bacon, and two pieces of toast, but Cathy Wade, I want you to eat all of it."

That afternoon, after a short visit with Doctor Williams, Cathy stopped by the pharmacy to pick up the prescriptions he had given her. He explained that she was suffering from the stresses of the missing plane, and as a result, he prescribed some medications to help her relax and to sleep. When she'd voiced her concern about becoming dependent on the drugs, the doctor had laughed and said, "Cathy, I have only ordered enough medication to last you two weeks. You are suffering from what we call situational stress, and the medication is justified with what is going on in your life right now. Additionally, if you do not abuse these meds, and take them only as directed, you have no need to worry about addiction."

Her next meeting, with her Pastor, was a much better meeting, as far as she was concerned. Pastor Lucas was an older man, with a small gut just starting to peek over his belt buckle, dark brown eyes, and a friendly smile on his face for everyone. While his hair had once been red, now it was streaked with strands of gray. He was married, had three children, and was actively involved in the community. He was a scout troop leader, ran the local community choir, and stayed busy helping kids with homework problems. Pastor Lucas was a man who looked, thought, and acted, as a pastor should, as far as Cathy was concerned.

They'd discussed Cathy's fears, and how God could help her in her time of need. Pastor Lucas promised that he'd have the whole church pray for her men, and that the hand of God sometimes worked wonders. But, he also reminded her that God didn't always make things turn out the way we want them to be. Cathy realized later, this simple, but open discussion with her pastor had the most calming effect on her.

He told her he would do his best to rally everyone to pray and assist her, yet ask them to respect her privacy at the same time. Both the pastor and Cathy knew most of the members of the church would want to call on her immediately to assist, but right now was not the time for visits. Pastor Lucas promised he would remind them to allow Cathy Wade time to determine what had happened to her son and husband, and then perhaps they could become more personally involved. They said a short prayer together and then she had driven home.

Cathy arrived home just before four, so she started dinner. She took one of the pills Doctor Williams had prescribed, and discovered it did not affect her mind much, other than relaxing her just a little. She was still very worried about Dave and Jim, but the deep anxiety she had carried the last few days disappeared.

Just as she was placing the beef roast into the oven, her front doorbell rang. She closed the oven and made her way to her door, wondering who might be visiting that time of the day. Upon unlocking and opening the door, she gave a loud laugh, and looked into the dark eyes of her daughter Marie as she asked, "Why didn't you just walk in, honey, like you always do?"

"I couldn't do that, mom. I left my keys on the dresser at the Colonel's house when I left for school this morning, and I didn't want to walk over there to get them. It's too cold to do much walking right now."

"Well, come on in. I'll have dinner done in about an hour."

"What are we having?"

"I've cooked your favorite, roast beef, with potatoes, carrots, celery, and onions. How does that sound?"

Marie sat at the table, lowered her head, and then asked in a low voice, "Mom, what do you think Dad and Davie are eating?"

Cathy kneeled beside her daughters chair, and raised her small chin with her right hand and spoke, "I think they're eating well, because you know how good

39

your dad is at hunting. And, remember, the airplane has a survival kit, and all of those kits have some food in them."

"Mom, I don't know if I can eat, because what if they don't have any food?"

"Marie, you and I have no control over what has happened to Dave or your Dad. We can only hope God protects them, and returns them to us unharmed. Right now, we have to take care of ourselves. Do you understand what I mean?"

"Sure, kind of."

"What don't you understand?"

"Mom, I'm scared. I mean, I fought with David all the time, and now that something might have happened to him, I feel terrible about it."

"Marie, listen to me honey, all brothers and sisters fight. They always have and always will. It's okay to argue; I even fought with your Uncle Ralph when we were growing up."

Marie gave a weak grin and asked, "You did?"

"Sure, and we fought all the time. So, I want you to forget about your fights with Dave. They were healthy fights, Marie. And, don't worry about what our men are eating. If I know your dad, they're mostly likely both sitting around a blazing fire right now, eating moose steaks!" Cathy said to her young daughter as she thought, *please God, feed my loved ones, now that they need you.*

CHAPTER 5

At that moment, Dave was thinking about eating, but it wasn't a steak from a moose. The young man was sitting near his fire, warming his hands, as a large chunk of fox meat roasted on a green stick over the fire. He had eaten some of the fox the night before, and didn't care much for the strong gamy tasting meat, but he had little choice. David knew he had to eat what was available and, at that moment, it was fox.

An earlier check of his traps had produced no new food, so he'd returned to camp, boiled a canteen cup of pine needle tea, and placed the meat on to roast. *Funny, I haven't had a soft drink in days, or any chips, either, and I don't miss either one of them. What I'd like right now is a big thick steak, and a salad with lots of veggies!* Dave thought as he reached over and rotated his meat over the coals.

After a few minutes, he pulled his wild tasting meat from the heat and took a small bite, making an ugly face unconsciously as he chewed it. As he ate he thought, *I'll take a look on the other side of the mountain this afternoon, and see what is out there. I doubt there is anything, but Dad said the Air Force used to have radar sites from World War 2 in this area. I don't think anyone would still be in one of them, but at least I'd have shelter and maybe a way to contact someone for help. I might even find a telephone that'll work!*

As soon as his meager meal of fox meat and pine needle tea was finished, Dave started cutting the meat he had on hand into thin strips. He had made jerky as a scout, and new the meat would last for years once it dried out. Due to the cold weather, he didn't fear his meat spoiling, but it would be easier to pack if he had to walk out. While his scout recipe called for lots of salt and pepper, both of which he lacked, he could make it without either of the spices. Also, in the scouts they had used an oven to dry the meat, so David wondered how it could be done in the bush.

He opened the damaged survival book, and on page 110 he noticed an illustration of how to dry meat by smoking. The illustration showed a tee-pee looking frame made of wood and a covering of parachute material. Inside of the frame were wooden racks that ran over a small fire at the base. He noticed the racks were high enough up that the flames from the fire could not touch them. David wondered what he could use to cover the frame, since he didn't have a parachute. It suddenly dawned on him; he could use the casualty blanket during the day to smoke meat, and then sleep with it at night. He quickly jumped to his feet and started working on a wooden frame.

Less than an hour later, David had a small frame constructed of green wood, and had his casualty blanket wrapped around it. Following the instructions in the survival manual, he then made a small fire at the base of his frame. He left a tiny opening at the top to allow the smoke from the fire to escape.

David then filled the drying racks inside the tee-pee with meat, and then closed the casualty blanket to allow the meat to dry. He had no idea how long it would take, but he knew it had taken over twelve hours when they had used his oven. He remembered once the meat had dried, it was lightweight and tasty. *Maybe drying the fox meat will make it taste better,* he thought as he glanced around his campsite.

He had run out of water at breakfast, so using his canteen cup, he packed it full of snow and placed it near his campfire. David knew not to put the cup on the hot coals or flames because the cup would get too hot, and the melted snow would become scorched, which left a bad taste. He had done it once on a hunting trip a few years before. He decided to melt enough water in his cup to fill the empty water bottles he had with him. The young man knew it would take hours, because he'd not only have to melt the snow, but allow the water to cool down enough to pour into the empty bottles without damaging them from the heat.

The morning and most of the afternoon passed slowly with David melting snow, filling his one-liter water bottles, and adding more wood to his tee-pee as the meat slowly dried. He felt a deep sense of accomplishment when he realized, for the first time since the crash, he was actually in control of what was going on around him. *Now,* he thought as he tightened the plastic cap on a water bottle, *if I can just get rescued.*

It was taking longer than he thought to smoke the meat, so he decided to look on the other side of the mountain the next day. His first priority was food and water, and then he could safely check the other side of the mountain. His father had always told him that a survivor must constantly make an effort find and prepare food in the bush. He had also stressed that any and all sources of food should be stored for rough times ahead; in case the weather turned bad or something happened to prevent the survivor from looking for food later.

At one point earlier in the afternoon, David heard the faint sound of an aircraft, but when he ran to the wreckage he could see nothing against the dark gray of the cloud cover over head. As the sound slowly disappeared, he suddenly felt a great loneliness settle upon him once more. As he stumbled back to his camp he thought, *They'll be back. They know Dad and I are missing, and they're looking for us. Next time, if they fly closer, I'll use the flare.*

It was late afternoon when David noticed movement in the trees. Knowing the country could contain everything from grizzly bears to rabbits, he picked up his rifle and chambered a round. He stood, and glancing toward the movement, he felt his heart beating fast in his chest, and each beat sounded like the big bass drum he'd played in the school band. For a second, he wondered if the animal could hear the pounding of his heart as clearly as he could.

Once again, he spotted movement, and the color seemed to be brown. As he held the gun in his shaking hands ready to fire, he knew real fear for the first time since the crash. If it was a bear, David knew he might be able to frighten it away, but then again, they were notional animals, and he might have to shoot it. He had grown up hearing tall tales of grizzly bears being shot ten times, and then walking back into the wilderness as if they had nothing more than a few mosquito bites. He didn't have the courage to face a grizzly, or so he thought. He flipped the rifles safety to the off position.

As Dave stood at the ready, the upper limps of a large pine moved, and out stepped a bull moose. *It must weigh well over a thousand pounds,* he thought as he felt his fear dissolve rapidly. The animal was meandering around the mountain eating, and David knew, deep inside, moose could still be very dangerous. For some reason it did not scare him like a grizzly bear would have. He'd heard stories of people attacked by moose, even on the Iditarod dog race from Anchorage to Nome, but a moose just didn't look vicious to the young man.

Knowing he might need meat in the future, if the weather turned to snow, David sighted his rifle on the area behind the big animal's right front leg, and slowly squeezed the trigger. The loud report of his rifle shot filled the air, and the moose dropped immediately in its tracks near a huge pine tree. David, having been warned about the danger of approaching an injured animal, quickly ejected the spent cartridge and chambered a fresh round.

The young man stood for almost ten minutes, ready to fire once more if the moose so much as twitched a muscle, but he noticed no movement at all. His Uncle Larry had told him on one hunting trip, "Son, when you shoot a big animal, always approach it from the rear. That away if the animal isn't dead, and tries to escape, you're not in its way. Many a hunter has been hurt by big animals only wanting to escape."

Walking toward the downed animal from the rear, David saw right off that the big beast was not breathing, and the chest was completely still. He suddenly felt sad he'd been forced to kill the magnificent looking creature, but he knew he had little choice if he wanted to survive. His emotions were a mess as he fought down the urge to cry out of sadness, and to shout for joy at the realization of the amount of meat he now had on hand.

David sat down on a large rock beside the pine tree and thought as he looked at the dead moose, *I'm sorry I had to kill you. If things had been different, I wouldn't have shot you. But, I need the meat, I really do. Please, forgive me.*

After a few minutes, David pulled his knife from his sheath and walked over to the fallen moose. He quickly gutted the large animal, keeping the liver and heart.

Due to the huge animal's size and weight, David had a very difficult time skinning it. Finally, after over two hours of struggling with it, he just removed the four large legs and took them back to his camp one at a time. Returning to the carcass, he removed as much of the meat as he could from the back, ribs and neck. *Well, I won't starve, that's for sure,* he thought, as he walked back to camp loaded down with dark red meat.

Since it was growing late, David placed the meat high up in the forks of a few trees around his campsite to keep small animals from stealing it from him. By the time he had finished it was dark and he was bone tired. He added a few small logs to his fire, stuck a large piece of liver on a green stick, and held it to cook over the hot coals. David was surprised that he had a strong desire for liver, which under normal circumstances he would never even consider touching. It was after he read part of the survival that he started to understand his unusual desire was the result of vitamins and minerals his body was losing as he attempted to stay alive. *There must be something in the meat I want, because my body is low on it.*

As soon as he had eaten, he checked his smoking meat, and found it was semi-dry, but not dry enough to be called jerky. He added a couple of small twigs to the fire, and then made his way back to his campfire, where he placed a canteen cup of pine needle tea on to boil. He still found the tea nasty, but it was better than nothing to drink. *Come morning, I'll have to start working on that moose meat. I'll bet I got six hundred pounds of meat, and I can't let it spoil on me. If the weather stays as cool as it has been, I'll be okay. But, all it will take is one warm day, and all that meat will be no good. I think tomorrow I'll make a good dozen more drying tee-pees, and start smoking that meat,* he thought, as his head lowered to his chest in exhaustion.

It was a little after two in the morning, when the old grizzly bear made his way toward the scent of fresh blood he'd picked up a little over an hour ago. While his eyesight was poor, his nose was excellent, and he had learned to depend on his nose and hearing much more than his eyes. Right now, his nose told him of a meal close by. He was old as grizzlies go, with his teeth no longer in good shape, and his body was sore each morning as he moved through the forests and mountains in search of food.

As a young bear, he'd often fed on slow or old caribou from large herds or the occasional deer or moose he'd find in the woods. As he aged, he found it more and more difficult to find enough to eat, because he was not as fast as he once had been. Earlier this day he'd torn a log to pieces feeding on ants, and while they were food, they hardly filled his huge empty stomach. It was a constant battle for him to find enough food to get fat so he could sleep through the long and rough Alaska winters. He thought of the delicious salmon he had fed on earlier this year, but the big fish were no longer in the fast running waters of his home range.

His pace was slow but steady as he moved in the direction his nose indicated the food was located. Suddenly he stopped. He picked up a scent he had not smelled in a very long time. It took him a few long minutes to correlate the smell with danger, but he had to eat, and knew he would face any danger at that moment to get a meal. Had he been able to think clearly, he would have known the scent was of man. The grizzly had only run into humans a few times in his long life, but each time they had hurt him severely, so he associated the scent with extreme danger.

The old bear walked to the carcass of the moose David had killed earlier in the day and started to feed immediately on the remains. His powerful jaws

47

snapped bones as if they were twigs as he ate. Spotting the gut pile, the large beast made his way to the discarded organs, and quickly ate all he could hold. Once full, the bear piled leaves and other debris on the carcass, and made his way back down the side of the mountain to find a place to sleep. He would return in the morning to continue his feast on the dead moose.

David was awakened by a loud sound, but he could not clearly identify it, though he knew it was close by. From what he could hear, something was moving near where he had killed the moose. He added another small log to his fire and pulled his rifle closer to him. At one point, he thought he had heard a low growl, but he was not sure if he really heard something or if it was just the wind. *Most likely it's a pack of wolves that have come to feed on the moose's body,* he thought as he relaxed a little. David, like most experienced Alaskans, knew wolves rarely if ever attacked humans. Besides, as long as he had his fire burning brightly he felt safe enough. The thought of a grizzly never entered his young mind.

Less than thirty minutes after hearing the noise, the young man was once more asleep. Since the night was warm enough, he slept beside the fire with little cover on him at all. As tired as he was, he didn't awaken until a false dawn was peeking over the mountain.

David opened his fanny pack, pulled out the last Meal Ready to Eat, noticing it was beef teriyaki, and opened the container. It was similar to the other meal, but only in packaging. He noticed his main pouch was indeed beef teriyaki, the side dish was chow mien noodles, but his biggest surprise was finding grape jam and a short bread cookie. He opened the accessory package and found an orange powdered drink, two small pieces of gum, a tea bag, and even a small book of matches. As he looked through the contents, he also found a pound cake, a moist towel to clean his hands, more hot sauce, salt, pepper, creamer, and toilet tissue.

As he picked up the toilet tissue he wondered, *why haven't I gone to do a number two yet? I've been out here for days now, and I don't have the urge at all. Must be the lack of a balanced diet, or maybe I'm eating too much meat.*

He pulled the survival manual open, but he could find nothing in the badly burnt book that talked about bowel movements or other health related subjects. He suspected that part of the book must have burned in the fire, but he made a mental note to start looking for plants that might help his body stay strong. Like most kids his age, David had been taught in school about health and the importance of the basic food groups, but he'd paid very little attention to the stuff because he found it boring. Now he wished he'd paid more attention.

As his teriyaki warmed up in the canteen cup of water, he opened the chow mien noodles and ate them. He enjoyed the crunchy tasting noodles, and was disappointed when he'd eaten them all. He considered opening the cake or the cookie, but instead he placed everything but the spork back in his fanny pack. He picked the spork up and realized the name was appropriate, for it was a fork and spoon rolled into one. The end of the spoon had little fork like tines, but they were not very long. At this point of his survival, David would have eaten his meal with his filthy fingers.

Opening the beef teriyaki pouch, he ate the warm meal slowly and enjoyed the thick sauce the most. Never in the past had he enjoyed a simple meal so much. Just like the last meal ready to eat, as soon as he'd eaten the contents, he cut the pouch open and licked the inside clean. He knew neither of his parents would approve of his manners, but he was hungry and did not intend to let even the smallest part of his meal escape. He then mixed the instant orange drink with the warm canteen cup water and sipped it slowly.

As soon as his meal was finished, David stood and placed his rifle over his right shoulder. He started toward the killed moose, intending to see what had caused the noise the night before. He suspected it was wolves, but he also knew it would be smart to see what had been at the animal's remains.

David took one look at the leaves and twigs thrown on the dead moose, and knew immediately he had a grizzly in the area. His Uncle Larry had been a serious bear hunter, and more than once he'd sat around a campfire at night explaining that grizzlies would usually cover a kill up, or at least partly, in an effort to hide it from other hungry animals.

As he neared the carcass, Dave saw the first track in the soil. The bears print was larger than David's foot, and that made an involuntary shudder run down the whole length of his spine. *That is one big griz, and I am not sure what to do now. I wonder if I should move my camp up higher, or maybe lower? Then again, maybe if I don't spook him or bother him he'll leave me alone,* he thought as he knelt and looked at the other prints of the large bear.

David quickly made his way back to this camp and stoked his fire back to life. He sat on the log and wondered about his next step. He didn't like the idea of having to move, especially with all the meat he had, but he didn't think he could kill a mad grizzly bear either. Finally, after much thought, he decided to stay where he was, and to continue smoking the meat.

Once his fire had burned down, David added fresh racks of meat to his tee-pee, placed a few small twigs on the little fire, and picked up his rifle. He had decided it was time to see what was on the other side of the mountain. Only this time, knowing a bear was in the area, he kept his rifle loaded and in his hands as he stepped into the trees.

Three hours later Dave was looking out over the tundra on the other side of the mountain. At first, he saw nothing, but then off in the distance he noticed a thin finger of smoke. His excitement grew, as he realized the smoke meant other people were near. But, as he stared at the smoke he wondered, *how far away were they? And, what kind of people could they be? Most likely,* he thought, *it is either some natives or a lone trapper out there. It's for sure not a town or anything very large or I'd know about it.*

As he slowly walked back to his camp, he was thinking about what he should do. He wondered if he should attempt to walk in the direction he'd seen the smoke or stay where he was. His father had often told him that in Alaska distances were confusing and what looked like a mile could end up being closer to five miles. Finally, he decided to think about it over night and decide in the morning. He knew very well that his decision could literally mean life or death.

Dave had just placed is rifle down on the log and added another log to his fire when he heard a movement to his right. Glancing up, he saw a huge grizzly bear standing on its hind legs sniffing the air. Panic filled the young boy, and he made a mad rush to pick up his rifle.

The bear, seeing the sudden movement, gave a bloodcurdling roar, dropped to all fours and charged straight at David.

CHAPTER 6

As the huge beast moved toward David, he aimed at the animal, and quickly pulled the trigger. While the grizzly had started his run straight toward the young man, at the sound of the loud rifle shot, the bear abruptly veered to the right and ran into the trees. David, acting from fear, attempted to move the bolt of his rifle up and back to load another round, but he only managed to drop the gun instead. Quickly bending over and picking the rifle up, he raised it and glanced around anxiously for the bear. The area around him was empty of any sign of the big animal.

The bear moved swiftly through the trees and up the side of the mountain. He was unsure why his shoulder burned and ached, but his one thought was to escape the loud noise. Each time he had heard that sound he'd been hurt by it, just as he had now. He was not sure what the scent and the noise had to do with his pain, but long ago, he had associated the smell of man with suffering.

Since his eyes sight was so poor, the bear had not seen David until he'd suddenly reached for the rifle, and any quick movement he thought must be food. Most animals, when they saw him, would attempt to run or move quickly to hide. He'd had no idea the movement was anything other than a meal. He'd smelled the scent of a human, just seconds before the quick movement, but due to the winds he was unsure where it was located.

The bear found a spot near the crest of the mountain and laid down to rest. His shoulder was throbbing now from pain, but he could not stop the hurting. He'd suffered gunshot wounds before, though he had no idea what they were. His temper was short and he felt a deep anger due to his throbbing, but there was nothing near for him to lash at in fury. He curled up in a ball and rested.

David slowly regained his composure. His legs were shaking and his hands trembling in an uncontrollable manner. He had never been so scared in his whole life, not even when he'd known the airplane was about to crash. The bear was so big and vicious looking as it charged him.

Taking his canteen cup, David filled it with water, placed it on the hot coals, and then pulled a tea bag from his Meals Ready to Eat. He also added another log to the fire, just in case the bear came back. He'd always heard animals were frightened of fire, but that bear had not acted like he'd even seen the flames.

I wonder if I shot that bear, he wondered as he placed the tea bag in the metal cup, *I hope not. I'm not sure if I wanted to kill it or just make him leave.*

The young man glanced up at the clouds, and could see another weather front moving in. Desperately he hoped it would snow. He'd heard bears and other large animals hibernated during cold weather, and he didn't ever want to see another grizzly bear in his life. He knew if it snowed he'd be able to sleep that night, but if the weather stayed clear he'd be up all night too terrified to sleep. Subconsciously, he placed another log on the fire, and looked out to the west where the sun was going down.

About an hour later, he was placing small twigs on the fire in his tee-pee filled with moose meat when the first snowflake struck him on his face. He smiled, closed the flap to the tee-pee, and walked back to his fire. Looking around, it was snowing, except it was coming down slowly. It was a typical snowfall for Alaska, and while Dave knew it would reduce rescue attempts, he still prayed for a storm that night.

For his dinner, he placed chunks of the moose heart and liver in the canteen cup and boiled it. After eating all of the rich meat, he drank the broth from his scanty meal. He then pulled out a pound cake, smeared some of the grape jelly on top of it, and had dessert. Though he felt content and relaxed, his rifle was never far from his side.

Snow was still falling, though there was very little on the ground. David knew this type of snow was lazy, and it might be morning before the ground was completely covered. He also knew, or at least he had heard some place, that when snow started falling, bears looked for a place to sleep. *I hope that's true. The last thing I need right now is a mad bear in this camp,* he thought, as he rearranged the logs in his fire to give off more light.

He wrapped the casualty blanket around his body, leaned back against the log, and watched the snow falling. At some point, he must have fallen asleep, because when he next opened his eyes the wind had picked up and the snow was falling with greater force. Glancing around, he noticed the snow was at least two inches deep in places and from the looks of the storm, he was sure to get a lot more. Part of the blanket had fallen open as he had slept, and he suddenly felt chilled. Adding another log to his fire, he moved back under the protection of the lower limbs of his pine tree shelter.

He suddenly remembered the last fishing trip he'd gone on with his father. They'd driven from Anchorage to Ninilchik, Alaska, and done some halibut fishing. The water had been rough, but the fish were feeding and they'd had a great time.

"I got a fish on, Dad!" David yelled with excitement, as he felt his line suddenly go taunt, and watched the tip of his rod start to dance.

"Keep the tip up, son, and reel him in slowly." His dad spoke in his usual calm voice, but David knew his father was excited too.

"Do you need help, son? Some of these halibut can go three hundred pounds or more." The boat captain asked as he walked over to where David was struggling with the fish.

"No . . . I want to . . . land this on my own," David replied, almost out of breath as he fought the heavy weight at the end of his line.

It took David about twenty minutes to bring the fish to the surface, and he was surprised when the boat captain reached down and struck the fish on the head with a club. After pulling the fish in with a gaff, the captain proudly said, "You have a fine catch son, well over sixty pounds."

"David, I'm proud of you. Just think, you did it all on your own, too, without any help at all!" His father had said, as he placed his arm around David's shoulder and gave him a big hug.

Suddenly, David felt tears running down his cheeks, and he glanced toward the wreckage of the airplane as he thought, *Why did you have to die, Dad? I love you, and I miss you. Dad, living like this is so hard for me. I'm trying not to let you down, but I don't know if I can take much more loneliness and fear.*

Knowing he was falling apart emotionally, David got up off the log, sliced some more of the moose meat, and checked the meat he had smoking in the tee-pee. Then, he returned to his campsite, and placed some of his wood under the large pine he used for a shelter to keep it dry. The young man knew from experience wet wood burned poorly, and smoked like all get out. Smoke seemed to always find a path into a person's eyes, and made them water.

It was very late before David finally wrapped up in the casualty blanket on the pine boughs under his tree and drifted off to sleep. He'd had a very rough day, and it had taken hours for the fear of the bear's charge to dissipate enough to allow him to sleep. He had just gone to sleep when he heard a plane flying over. Usually he would have rushed to the wreckage, only he knew he would see nothing in the poor light. This time David didn't even get out of bed and run to the wreckage; he knew he was too late.

Morning dawned cold, but the snow had quit. David saw less than three inches on the ground, as he warmed up some pine needle tea in his cup. *Today I need to try to get out of here, he thought, as the flames from the fire brought his water to a boil. I'll head toward the smoke I saw, and hope it's a native village or maybe a trapper. I can't stay here, not when I know there are other people around. But, before I go, I need to make sure the smoke I saw is still there. It could have been someone moving through the area, and all my walking would then be for nothing. If the smoke is still there later this morning, I'll head that way before noon.*

After a quick breakfast of more moose meat and his tea, David made his way up the side of the mountain. He was very cautious as he glanced around, hoping the big bear had left the area. David also made a lot of noise, hoping to scare the bear if it was nearby. The trail upward was a little more difficult, due to the new snow, but in less than two hours after leaving his camp, David stood on the side of the mountain and could see the thin finger of smoke off to the west. *I need to get back to camp, pack up my gear, and get on the trail. I may have to spend a night or two on the trail before I reach where that smoke is located,* he thought as he shifted the rifle from his right hand to his left.

Less than an hour later, David had returned to camp, packed up his gear, and started moving down the side of the mountain. He had made a rough looking sled from the sheet metal he had used for his fire, along with some rope from the survival kit, so he could pulled some of his moose meat over the snow. Once he reached the flat land, he knew the going would become easier. He quickly located an animal trail that led down the side of the mountain, but it meandered in all directions, which meant it would take him a lot longer to reach the base. The going was slow, and he had to be cautious not to slip on the steep trail. The last thing he needed was a broken leg or other injuries.

His right leg, where he'd been cut during the crash of the airplane, was healing nicely, and David was concerned about opening it up again if he fell. He thought of his father, still trapped in the wreckage of the plane, but forced himself to concentrate on what he was doing, so he wouldn't get depressed again. His father wanted him to live, so David decided he'd give it his best shot.

By mid morning, he had still not reached the base of the mountain, as large snowflakes began to fall and the wind picked up. Dark gray clouds were close enough overhead, that David thought he could actually reach up and touch them, but what concerned him the most was the simple fact he knew no rescue aircraft would be flying in such cloud cover. Well, he thought as he stepped over a log on the trail, *I'll just have to move a little faster and get to where I saw that smoke. I'll need to keep from sweating though, or I'll be in serious trouble. No, I don't think other people would be out in this weather. It looks like a storm might be coming, so I'd better find shelter.*

David located some protection from the wind back in a thick group of trees, and soon had a shelter constructed of pine boughs. Using his flint and steel, he started a fire, sliced off small pieces of moose meat, and set it to boil in his canteen cup. The snow was coming down faster now, and the young boy knew the temperature had dropped at least twenty degrees since he'd moved into the trees. As he sipped the broth from his meat, he thought, *big storm coming. I'm not so sure I made the right decision to move when I did. It might have been smarter to stay near the airplane, but it's too late to change my mind now. I'll wait this storm out, and then move toward the smoke again.*

The sky grew almost black as the sun was blocked out by the storm, but David had seen it happen many times in the past, though he'd always had a safe place to watch storms before. He was concerned by the storm, but not actually scared of it. He remembered his father telling him that in a snowstorm, the key was to keep warm, stay dry, and to have a shelter. David had those things, except he was impatient to be moving toward the smoke he'd spotted. *I need to use some common sense here,* he thought, as he added a small piece of wood to his fire, *or I'll end up dying before I ever see where that smoke came from. I need to keep my head screwed on right, and take this slowly.*

Four hours later the snow was knee deep, the wind was howling in the darkness, and David Wade was huddled up in his shelter shivering with the cold. While the space blanket kept him warm, he was still cold, but on the inside. It was then he remembered a warning he'd heard over a campfire one night a few years before, "Never sleep in really cold weather with the same clothes on you've been traveling in, because they'll be damp from your sweat. And if you feel super cold inside you need a hot drink." *I don't have any choice on the clothes matter,* David thought as he added some water to his canteen cup, and dropped some pine needs in, *but I might as well drink something hot. That might help warm me up a little.*

Sucking on a single piece of hard candy as he sipped on his hot pine needle tea, he stopped shivering, and David realized his body was cold because he was running out of energy. He remembered when his class had gone on cross-country ski meets, the teacher always made them take candy along, because the sugar gave each skier an extra boost of energy in the deep cold. He couldn't remember why the sugar helped, he'd not paid much attention when the teacher explained it, but it worked, and for that he was very thankful.

By midnight, the snow had died down, but the temperature was well below zero with the wind-chill. The top of Dave's shelter was covered with snow, and while the inside was not warm by any means, it was much warmer than outside. There was no wind at all inside, so all he needed to do was keep covered up with his casualty blanket. His fire had died and was now covered with freshly fallen snow. The young man had camped in the snow before, and he'd made lots of fires in snow, so he knew as soon as it got daylight he needed a small platform of logs to keep his new fire from sinking into the snow once lit. He'd beat the snow down, lay his platform, and then start his fire, but he'd need to keep some other logs around to replace the ones on the platform that burned as his fire burned.

David sat in his shelter, listening to the wind howling, and suddenly started to cry. He felt a deep pain when he remembered his father's warm smile, and how he had always been understanding with him when he had problems, or got into trouble. The young boy shuddered, gave a loud moan, and whispered, "Dad, oh, Dad. . . I never thought something like this would ever happen to us. I miss you, and I can't imagine spending the rest of my life without you." Then, suddenly he felt an inner sense of pure determination hit him, as if someone had flipped a switch on in his mind, and knew he would survive! He had to survive! David knew at that exact moment his self pity and mourning for his father had to stop until rescue, because he felt close to breaking down.

David, never one to pay much attention in church or Sunday school, raised his head, looked out at the lightly blowing snow and said, "God, you have my father now, so please tell him I'm trying my best to survive. Let him know, God, that I'm fine and miss him. I know I've not been a perfect person, especially in school or when I fight with Marie, but I'll try to change if I survive this. I need your help, and I need it soon, God, because I'm so alone. Please, help me God. Amen."

CHAPTER 7

The snow was falling hard in Anchorage, and the temperature was five below zero as David's mother finished shopping and walked out to her car. As she unlocked the door to her car, she suddenly wondered if her two lost men were safe and warm. She had little concern about their actual survival, if James and David were unhurt, because she'd seen her husband in the woods and he was more at home there than in his own home. Cathy started the car and then sat for a few minutes as she waited for the fog on the glass of the vehicle to clear so she could see well enough to drive. As the heater warmed up, she prayed Jim and Dave had a fire and enough protection from the cold to keep them alive. As she had said many times since she had been notified the plane was missing, *it's the waiting that's the most difficult part,* she thought as she pulled from her parking spot, *the not knowing one way or the other.*

Pulling into her garage, Cathy took the groceries and walked through the door into the kitchen. She immediately noticed the house smelled of fresh bread and the smell had always brought a comment from Dave about how good it smelled. A couple of years before, Jim had bought her a bread machine and at least three times a week Cathy made fresh bread for the family. She remembered setting the timer on the machine so the bread would bake while she was out. *The smell of fresh bread baking always makes a house smell like a home,* she thought with a weak smile as she opened the door to her cupboard and started putting her dried and canned groceries away.

She had just placed the last package of meat in the freezer when the phone rang. Cathy hurried to the kitchen, picked up the phone and answered, "Wade residence, Cathy speaking."

"Cathy, Frank Wilcox here. I'm in the command post and we've been very busy the last hour or so."

"Frank, I hate to ask, but anything new?" As Cathy asked, she was not sure she was ready for the answer.

"Some, but not much. A little over two hours ago a commercial airliner flying near where Jim went down reported hearing an emergency locator beacon for a few minutes on the guard frequency. The pilot claimed it lasted for only a minute or two, and then it gradually grew weaker until it died."

Cathy thought for a minute and they asked, "So what does that mean to us, Frank?"

"Cathy, only one plane has ever disappeared in the area we suspect Jim went down. We know where most crashes have occurred in the past and we keep them marked on a map here at the rescue center. It had to be the E.L.T. from Jim's plane."

"Does that mean you have good news, then?"

Frank Wilcox hesitated for a few seconds and then spoke, "Cathy, what it means is, we have a better idea where the crash site is, or so I suspect. It does not mean that either Jim or Dave survived the crash, only that the emergency beacon came on for a short period. However, the pilot gave us the map coordinates and we know, within a little distance, where the beacon is."

"What now?"

Frank hesitated, knowing Cathy wanted to know one way or the other, but the weather was so severe his choppers were grounded. Finally, he said, "As soon as there is a break in the weather my men will go out. I actually had to order a few of my pilots not to go out, as it is. Jim is a well-liked man, Cathy, and many of my aircrew members know him very well. But, I cannot allow them to fly in a storm like this or I'll end up searching for some of them as well."

"Any idea when this weather will break?"

Frank cleared his throat and then said, "My weather guys tell me not before three or four more days. The front is a long one that is moving in from Russia, and they expect as much as forty inches of snow on the ground by the time it quits."

"T. . . thanks for the call Frank." Cathy spoke as she realized this storm could end up killing both Jim and Dave.

"Cathy, I promise you, the first chance my boys get to fly they'll be out and at the location we have from the airliner. I suspect they can be there, inspect the crash site, and let us know what they find within two hours or so. Right now, all we can do is hope for a break in the weather. I'll call you again as soon as something starts to happen around here."

"Bye Frank, and thanks." Cathy quivered with the news as she placed the phone back on the charger.

Forty inches of snow and the plane down in the mountains! She thought as she stood in the kitchen unsure what to do next.

* * *

Colonel Frank Wilcox was concerned. The weather had been bad for the last twelve hours and he knew from experience; even if Jim and Dave had survived the crash, a long lasting blizzard of the sorts often seen in Alaska could kill them both. While the colonel had faith in Jim's survival skills, even the most qualified individuals could very easily die if the weather got too rough. Knowledge, without the proper equipment, could only keep a person alive for so long. Of course, he thought as he picked up the phone, *a lot depends on their physical conditions,* but he spoke into the phone, "Give me weather."

"Weather, Senior Master Sergeant Wilson speaking." The voice from the weather shop answered a second later.

"Sergeant Wilson, this is Colonel Wilcox of SAR, what's the forecast for the next forty-eight hours or so?"

"Wait one, sir, I'll check."

As Wilcox waited, Senior Master Sergeant Donaldson brought him a cup of hot coffee and placed it on his desk. The Sergeant knew the Colonel had been up all night locating the beacon location on the map and talking to the commercial pilot on the phone. It had taken hours because they had to track the pilot down in a hotel in Tokyo, Japan where he was resting over night.

"Sir, Sergeant Wilson speaking, it's not very good for the next few days, I'm afraid. The next forty-eight to seventy-two hours will be pretty much what we have out there right now. According to Captain Carter, my OIC, the weather might have a slight break about twenty-four hours from now, but that break will most likely last less than four hours."

"Thanks Sergeant Wilson, I appreciate the report."

"Any time Colonel, and feel free to give us a call."

As he hung up the phone, Wilcox wondered if the weather break the forecasters were calling for would really happen. *Four hours would be cutting it close, but I've got to do something. I'll see if Zlotkowski and Baldwin will fly the mission. If they'll risk the flight, I'll give the go ahead, but the weather will have to be clear,* he thought as he stood from his chair and stretched his sore and tired muscles.

He picked up the phone once more, dialed a number and said, "Give me Zlotkowski."

A couple of minutes later a voice said, "Captain Zlotkowski speaking."

"Zee, this is Colonel Wilcox. I need you and Baldwin on standby starting at midnight tonight. Contact your crew and put them on alert as well. The weather guys are projecting a small window of good weather at about this time tomorrow and if it happens, you're going out to find Doctor Wade."

"Roger that sir, we'll be ready to go when you give the call. But, I'll need to send Baldwin over to get what information you have on the crash site, or better yet, could you send your mission planner over with the details? That way my whole crew can listen in on the briefing."

"No problem Zee, I'll get Captain Parker to come over in a couple of hours and brief your crew. You call back, speak to Parker and let him know when your crew is at the alert shack. But, Zee, this could be a very dangerous flight and if you don't want it, when the time comes you tell me, Okay?"

Captain John Zlotkowski laughed and replied, "Colonel, we train for rough missions, so we should be ready for this. And, I promise you, if I think my crew cannot do the job I'll let you know. How's that, sir?"

"Fine John, I'll leave the acceptance of the mission, or the declining up to you."

"Well, send your man over after I call back and we'll see what we can do about getting the good doc out of the woods."

"Alright, Zee." Colonel Wilcox put the phone down and wondered where the Air Force came up with good men like Zlotkowski and his crew. They were always ready for the dangers and challenges of a rescue mission, regardless of the risks, any time.

When Sergeant Donaldson entered the colonel's office with some routine messages, the old Sergeant gave Wilcox the eye, grinned and said, "With all due respect sir, but you look a complete mess. Why don't you go and get some sleep and let me hold the fort down?"

Wilcox yawned, rubbed his tired eyes and replied, "I'll do that Sarge, and I'll be at my home if you need me. Also, get a weather check every four hours from the weather guys. Any break in the weather coming, you call me immediately regardless of the time of day. Oh, and when Captain Zlotkowski calls, let him speak to Parker. I want Parker to go to the alert shack and give Zee's crew a mission briefing on the Wade plane."

"Yes sir, I'll keep a close eye on the weather for you and I'll pass on to Captain Parker to expect a call from Captain Zlotkowski."

Wilcox picked up his fatigue cap and left his office. He was near the door to the main building when he heard a voice call his name and turning, he noticed it was General Moores.

"Frank, I was just returning to my office from a staff meeting, do you have a few minutes?" The General asked as he gave Colonel Wilcox a very sober look.

"Sure sir." Frank Wilcox replied and then thought, *what does he expect me to say when he wears two stars and wants to see me? I have little choice, I'd say.*

As they entered the General's office the senior officer said, "Close the door and be seated, Frank. This conversation, well, let me say it's not one I want to have with you. The search for Doctor Wade and his son will have to be called off by the end of the week. I got a message in from the Search and Rescue Center at Scott Air Force Base and they have two reasons for calling this to an end."

Wilcox waited, knowing the senior officer had more to say, but dreading every single word he would hear.

"First, the survival experts don't think those two could survive in this kind of weather for over ten days, and that's how long it will be this Friday. Furthermore, they pointed out to me that as the rescue proceeds we are using up valuable fuel, time, and resources. I know that you are of friend of the Wade family, but Frank, we have to draw a line and the four star General at Headquarters Air Force has drawn it for me." The General spoke slowly as he walked to the window with his hands locked behind his back and looked out at the falling snow.

Colonel Frank Wilcox didn't comment; he simply closed his tired eyes as he wondered how he would be able to tell Cathy Wade.

"Come on, Frank, what's on your mind? I've known you too long not to know you have something to say." The General said as he walked to his desk and sat down in his oversized chair.

"General Moores, has this all been coordinated with the Civil Air Patrol and the civilian volunteers who are involved with the search?"

The older man met Frank's eyes and replied, "No, of course not. I wanted to explain it to you before I informed anyone. You're the best I've ever seen in the rescue business, Frank, and I mean that. But, don't let your personal involvement with this missing man and his family cloud your judgment. You and I both know that in search and rescue the most important time is the first forty-eight hours and with each hour after that the chances of finding a survivor alive goes down."

"Sir, you and I are both flyers. You know as well as I do that there are times when folks have lived much longer than ten days in the bush."

"Frank, this is not like a combat search and rescue mission where we quickly fly in and recover the man, or he gets captured within a few hours by the enemy. While James Wade was a good pilot, he didn't have near the flying time either of us has and, I hate to say this, it's more than likely they are both dead. My God, Frank, it must be twenty below out there right now!"

"But, I have the General's permission to search up until midnight on Friday, is that correct sir?"

General Moores gave a dry chuckle and as he spoke his eyes turn stern, "You can do that Frank, but on one condition. I want no aircrew lives put in danger with this mission. If, and I mean if, the weather breaks you can launch your birds, but no launches in bad weather."

Frank stood, saluted the General, and did an about face to leave the room. Just as he was reaching for the door, he heard General Moores say, "Frank, I'm sorry about this. I know how hard it must be for you, and if I can help in any way, just let me know. Now, go and get some rest, you look like something two cats dragged in."

As Frank Wilcox drove home he kept thinking, *I've only got five days left to find Jim and Dave. I won't tell Cathy Wade about the deadline until Thursday, because if I tell her now it will just cause her to worry more. Why in the world did I ever get into this business?* A few miles down the road, he answered his own question as he thought, *because sometimes we save lives.*

Frank kissed and hugged his wife, glanced briefly at the mail, and took a long hot shower. Quickly changing into his pajamas, he ate his dinner at the kitchen table as he talked about the rescue in general terms with his wife. One thing Frank had learned after almost twenty-five years of marriage was to keep his work to himself, or at least the dangerous or critical aspects of the job. He didn't want her to worry and he for sure wasn't going to tell her about his discussion with General Moores, because he was just too tired to try to explain the logic behind the decision for the deadline.

He finished eating and taking his coffee, he walked to the sofa in front of the fireplace. He placed his tired feet up on the coffee table. As the fire cracked and popped, he wondered if Jim or Dave were still alive. He knew Jim was no quitter and Dave was cut from the same cloth, because the boy had always done well on any hunting trip. *Listen to me, if you both are alive, or even just one of you, hang tough, because I'm coming for you as soon as I can,* Frank thought as he raised his coffee cup to his lips.

By the time Carol had showered and dressed, Frank was asleep on the sofa. She covered him gently with a blanket, turned the television down low, and curled up beside him. While Frank had not said anything she knew the military was about to call the search and rescue mission off because of weather and besides, she'd been married to the man too long not to know when something serious was on his mind. But, anyone would have serious doubts of finding survivors after weather like this. *You're a good man and I know you'll hate breakin' the news to Cathy, but you'll do it if it comes to that. That's one of the things I love about you, Frank, you always do what is best, whether you like doing it or not,* Carol thought as she picked up the remote and started channel surfing.

CHAPTER 8

D avid didn't know the snow had stopped a little after midnight, because he had fallen asleep shortly after his prayer. For an hour or so, even the moon was out as it peeked through the cloud cover. While Dave slept, a small pack of wolves moved silently across the soft new snow, drawn to the smell of well over a hundred pounds of dried meat the young boy had in his shelter. The wind had died down, though the temperature was still well below zero, and while the snow had quit, it was only for a short while.

The dried moose meat was in the back of Dave's shelter. He had packed the meat in the remains of three slightly burned sweaters from his shelter fire, to protect it from the wet snow. This night he was actually using the meat as a rough pillow as he slept. The young boy awoke as his head hit the snow and it took him a few seconds to clear the grogginess of deep sleep from his mind. Seeing movement near the entrance of his shelter, he glanced at a motion and instantly recognized the form of a wolf.

David saw one of his sweaters of dried of meat in the wolf's teeth, so the young man reached out with both hands and grasped the garment. Instantly there came a low growl from the hungry wolf and the animal began to rock its head from side to side in an attempt to pull the meat from the young man. Dave pulled with

73

all of his might and the sweater suddenly pulled free, but he fell on his back and lost his grip on the meat.

Remembering his rifle, David reached for the gun just as the big wolf bared his teeth, gave another low growl, and quickly snatched the sweater full of meat. As the animal turned to run away, Dave brought his rifle up, but due to the darkness, he was unable to see his sights. "Give me back my meat!" The boy screamed as he pulled the trigger on the rifle and exited his shelter.

David saw a few pieces of dried moose meat laying in the snow, so he quickly picked them up and put them in his butt-pack. He had never considered an animal would be out in the snow like this, mainly because when he had gone to sleep the snow was falling hard and fast. The wolves, along with his sweaters of meat, were now long gone, into the countryside. Glancing around, he saw no blood on the snow, so he knew he'd missed the hungry animal when he'd shot.

Now, what do I do? He thought, as he kneeled by his dead fire and quickly started making a new one, *I have no more meat. I should have thought of wolves, but I didn't and the mistake cost me dearly. All that work just to let a pack of wolves have it!*

As he built his fire, he remembered what one elderly hunting guide had said to him one night when they were up north looking for caribou. One evening during the trip, David had heard the long drawn out howl of a wolf and he had asked the man if wolves ever attacked people. The old guide had grinned and said, "Well, now, son, not that I've ever heard tell of, but I've only lived in Alaska for nearly fifty years. I do know though, a wolf will steal you blind of any meat you leave laying around or other foods not in a sealed container. And, a pack of wolves is a fearsome sight to see and I've seen lots of 'em, but I've never heard of a wolf pack ever attacking a healthy man. I suspect if that man was almost dead they might attack 'em, only I ain't real sure. All that stuff you see in the movies 'bout fellers out campin' and the wolves attacking is pure nonsense, boy."

David added a larger piece of wood to his fire and thought, *No, they didn't attack me or even try to hurt me. The wolves only wanted my meat. From now on, if I get any more meat, I'll have to hang it up high in a tree or guard it all night. And, I need to keep my rifle where I always know where it is. If that had been a grizzly bear instead of wolves, I might be dead right now.*

It was close to an hour later before the young man grew sleepy once more and made his way back inside his shelter. He placed his rifle at his right side, wrapped up in his blanket, and promptly fell asleep. No sooner had David closed his tired eyes than the snow started to fall once again and the fire snapped and crackled as the wet snowflakes struck.

Morning dawned extremely cold with snow still falling. The flakes were falling slowly and the wind had all but died completely. David stood, stretched, and made his way to his snow covered and dead fire. Within a few minutes his fire was burning well, a canteen cup of pine needle tea was boiling, and the young man nibbled on one of the pieces of dried moose meat he had been able to save. He glanced up at the sky and knew there would be no rescue aircraft out in the thick overcast clouds above. *I'll eat, drink my tea, and then be on my way again. I hope the place where I saw the smoke is not too far away, because I only have a little food left,* he thought as he stirred his tea with a clean piece of wood.

As soon as his skimpy meal was finished, David packed his blanket in his butt pack, and started his way down the mountain. If he was lucky he'd be at the base before noon, then all he had to do was cross a few miles of open country and he'd be where he'd seen the smoke. While he walked, he wondered if the smoke was from a lone trapper, or perhaps a small village of natives. He knew in Alaska it could be either and it would not have surprised him to discover the smoke came from a trapper who also happened to be a native. If you named a group of people in Alaska, each of them had some that trapped, worked as hunting guides, or fishing guides. David thought about native Alaskans for a few minutes as he made good time going down the trail.

In his school, there were some native kids and Dave had always gotten along well with most of them. Some of the kids he'd known had given the native Alaskan kids a real hard time and he could not really understand why. As far as he was concerned, he had seen no big differences in any of the kids he'd gone to school with. Well, of course, some were of different colors, or some spoke a different language at times, but the real differences as far as he was concerned were small. He asked his mother about it once at the breakfast table.

"David, most people, regardless of their color or language are looking for the same things out of life. Now, some may place more importance on certain things than others do, but overall we're all similar."

"I don't understand what you mean." David said as he picked up his fork and took a bite of his egg.

"Well, all people have a basic desire for food, clothing, shelter, friends, and a good job. But, some may want to have more money, so they might be tightfisted over spending too much, so they can save. Others, perhaps, may stress the importance of a healthy family and then control what foods they eat or even force the whole family to exercise. Some, like ours, may want a church or temple to be part of their lives and they may be very active in religion."

"I think I understand, but I get confused at school when some of my friends won't let someone else in our group because they're a different color."

His mother laughed, leaned forward and asked, "Do you think the color of a person makes them good or bad?"

"I am not sure what I think."

"David, there are all kinds of people running around in the world today. There are good people and there are bad ones. Each race has its fair share of bad and good people. Always remember to judge a person by their behaviors and not by their color. See, the attitude of judging based on color goes way back, long before America was discovered. Surprisingly, that ugly attitude applies in all races and it has happened in all countries. In some countries years ago, if you were not of the dominate color, then you were either a slave or looked down on. It didn't matter what color the majority were either, black, white, Asian, all of them did it."

"Is that why the Civil War was fought?" David asked, thinking he finally understood.

His mother gave a warm laugh and replied, "No, not just for that reason, I guess. The issues behind the Civil War are complex and hard to explain over a quick breakfast. But, slavery was only one of the issues, just as states' rights were, and you are correct about the importance of color in those days. Anyone who was not white was considered a slave or looked down on. It still happens is our society today, only it's covered up very well and not as open. I think you just saw some of it at school with your friends. You, young man, just remember that each person has a soul, can think, has feelings, and deserves your respect until they do something wrong. Now, eat your breakfast and be out that door in a few minutes for school, or you'll be late."

As Dave walked and thought over the conversation, he realized his mother was right. He was sure anyone, regardless of their color or the language they spoke, would want the same things he did right here and now. They would want food, shelter, warmth, and to be rescued. The more he thought about it the more he realized his friends had been wrong in judging people as they had. He could understand how a group could only want others like them in the group, but that didn't make the group right. Dave almost slipped and fell at that point, so he concentrated on his trail and quit thinking about others.

The young man walked from the mountain near noon and faced an open snow covered plain. Pulling his compass from his fanny pack, David watched the black arrow spin and then stop, pointing north. While not anywhere near an expert with a compass, he did know how to use one to a certain point. As far as Dave was concerned, it mattered little that he didn't have a map, because he didn't know how to read one anyway. The dial had numbers on it and by looking at the numbers, if the compass needle pointed to the north, he had a heading or so he thought. When he'd been on the mountain, he had taken a compass heading of the smoke so he moved off on a west by north route.

His compass, which he had stuck in his right coat pocket, fell from his coat as he bent down to tie his boot laces a few minutes later. The young boy didn't notice the loss for over an hour when he stopped to take another reading. He frantically searched for the compass, but it was not there. David considered going back for it, but when he turned to look at his back trail the wind and blowing snow had covered most of his tracks, so he knew the compass was long buried in snow.

Most the day David kept his heading as well as he could. With the low clouds, the only way he could keep his bearing was to keep the mountain he had been on in view and at the same location. By keeping the mountain over his left shoulder, he knew he was still heading the right way. My mid-afternoon the snow started falling heavily once more and it became too difficult for him to continue walking, but since he was still in the open, he stopped to consider a shelter. *I guess I'll have to make a snow shelter of some kind,* he thought as he looked around and quickly noticed there were no trees, hills, or any natural shelters he could see. He had made a snow trench once with his father in the back yard.

Using the aluminum sled he'd had his moose meat on, he scooped some snow out and made a long trench about three feet deep. He widened it, so it was almost two feet wide and six feet long, but he didn't have a top to keep the snow out. He paused when the task was completed and wondered, *how do I cover the top of this thing? There isn't a tree for miles and I only have my casualty blanket. I can't use the blanket, because I'll freeze without it. I know! I use blocks of snow!*

David tried using his sheath knife to cut the snow, but the blade was too short, so as he looked around for a better tool, it dawned on him to use the aluminum he used for a sled. He straightened the metal and it worked fine, though his first blocks were too thin and fell apart when he attempted to pick them up. After attempting a few different thicknesses of snow, he finally discovered that a block about ten inches thick worked fine. He quickly covered his shelter and crawled inside with all of his equipment. The entrance to his shelter he covered with the aluminum from the sled.

The young boy had only been in his shelter for a little less than an hour when he suddenly developed a bad headache. He opened his fanny-pack, pulled out the minimum first aid kit, and took two of the pills for headaches. Dave was well aware of the dangers of taking any medicine because his father had often warned him of the risks of even over the counter medications. His dad had said adult painkillers were especially dangerous for children. David felt he had little choice because his head was pounding.

No sooner had he taken the medication, than Dave remembered a conversation that had taken place a few years earlier, when he'd attempted to make an igloo in the back yard. He had been able to construct most of the igloo, but he was unable to get the final block in place. Each time he'd attempted to place the last block for the igloo into position it collapsed and he could not figure out why.

Finally, his father had walked up, smiled, and said, "Igloos are not easy to make, Dave. And, as you've learned, the final block is the hardest to put into place."

"Dad," David has replied as he glanced up at his father as he started cutting another block of snow, "how do the Eskimos do it then?"

His father laughed and said, "They don't make igloos much anymore. Oh, I suspect some of them still know how it's done, but most of the old ways are gone or quickly disappearing. Most folks just dig a trench shelter and throw a tarp over it and cover it with snow."

"Why would the old ways disappear?"

"Dave, with contact with the white man, some of the natives of Alaska have changed in ways we can't even begin to imagine. Now they have snow machines, wooden homes, skis, aluminum boats, and the list goes on. So, all of that has changed the needs of the people as well. Most of the time now, a native will throw up a tent or use a tarp for a shelter, or as I said, makes a snow trench to keep warm in."

"I guess the change is good for them, huh?"

His father thought for a few seconds and then replied, "Who is to say if it's good for them or not. I guess it has made their lives a little easier, but it's sad to see the old ways die."

"Is a snow trench hard to make?"

"Huh-uh, a trench shelter is not hard at all, Dave. You just dig a long trench, cover it with a tarp, pine boughs, or whatever you have on hand, and you're done. But, always remember to keep a hole in your shelter, so you have ventilation."

Suddenly, the thought of ventilation struck Dave, and he suspected what had caused his headache, the lack of fresh air. Taking his knife, Dave cut a hole about three inches in diameter and made a ventilation hole. Within a few minutes, his headache disappeared. Feeling much better, the young man pulled an energy bar from his fanny-pack and slowly nibbled at it. He was hungry, but he suspected a lot of his hunger was because he knew he didn't have any food left, not to really speak of except a little meat. He had one more piece of dried moose meat and one energy bar and that was it.

What David really wanted and needed was a hot drink, but he couldn't think of a way to make a fire. While he had a way to light a fire, he had nothing that would burn long enough to allow him to boil water. He considered the survival book, but since it was paper he knew it wouldn't last long enough to make his water boil, nor would anything else he had with him. Instead of a hot drink, the young man stuck a piece of hard candy in his mouth and waited for it to melt. He knew the sugar in the sweet would give him some energy and help raise his body temperature, but he knew he was in for a long and cold night.

All night long, Dave heard the wind howling just outside of his shelter and at one point he became scared of being buried alive. *What if so much snow falls I can't get out in the morning?* He thought as he rolled over to get more comfortable, except then remembered he had his sheath knife, so he could always dig his way out. At times off and on, he'd take the blade of his knife and poke it through the hole he had for ventilation. He wanted to make sure he continued to breathe clean and fresh air.

It was many long hours later before Dave noticed the light from his ventilation hole had grown from black to a light gray. He was shivering from the cold and knew he had to get up and continue moving toward the smoke he had seen. At least as he moved he had been warm and though he had survived a bad blizzard, the young man felt anything but lucky. When he pushed the metal away from the entrance to his shelter, he noticed it was difficult to move, but after a few minutes of struggling, it fell to the side.

As soon as he stuck his head from the shelter, he saw the overcast sky with low gray clouds and the threat of more snow. As soon as he had crawled from his shelter, he stood, stretched, and felt his whole body ache. He was sure some of his body pain was still from the airplane crash, though he suspected most of it came from sleeping poorly in the cramped spaces of his shelter.

David snapped the fanny-pack around his waist, and remembering the sunglasses in his coat pocket, he pulled them out and put them on. While the sun showed no hint of making an appearance at all this day, he felt the glasses might cut down on the wind in his eyes. The day before the blowing wind had caused some irritation to his eyes, and he wanted to prevent that from happening again, if he could. Taking one quick glance around the open nothingness that surrounded him, he moved off once more, keeping the mountain over his shoulder.

The snow was mid-calf deep and every few minutes the young man had to stop and rest to avoid overheating. By the end of the day, both legs ached and he was very hungry. It had taken all of the will power he had not to eat the last energy bar he had in his pack. The only positive aspect of the whole day he could see, as it began to grow dark, was he now had a campsite in a thin grove of trees. As well as he could tell when he decided to stop for the night, the trees grew thicker a little further along, but he was simply too exhausted to go on. He quickly gathered some firewood, started a small fire, and made a crude shelter using the limbs from some of the smaller trees. With his shelter and fire taken care of, David sat on a small log to relax. It had been a very tiring day for him.

As his canteen cup of pine needle tea boiled on the hot coals of the fire, he felt a pain in his right foot, near the toes. He removed his boot and was surprised to find the flesh white and shriveled up as if he'd been in the bathtub too long. The cause of his pain was cracked skin under his middle toe. Unsure what to do, he took his boot from the other foot and placed them both to dry near the fire, resting both feet on his boots. He wished he had some clean and dry socks to put on, but they had burned in his shelter fire. Instead, he laid his damp socks on his pack near enough to the fire to heat, but not burn.

The snow had started again, but it was once more a lazy snow and it didn't concern him nearly as much as the blizzard the day before. While he was still very much alone, there was comfort in having a fire and being in the trees. As he placed another log on his small fire he thought, *I wonder what my mom and sister are doing right now? I'll bet they are having a great meal and are worried about us.* Dave never felt the wet tears run down his cold cheeks as he unconsciously stared into the dancing flames of his fire.

His only answer was the snapping of the damp wood as it dried in the flames.

CHAPTER 9

"Colonel Wilcox, this is Sergeant Barnes with the weather shop. I was asked to inform you that the weather break we have will last close to five hours." A voice on the phone said to Frank Wilcox as he sat at his desk.

"Thank God, and thank you as well, Barnes." Wilcox spoke, hung up and dialed the number to the alert shack.

"Captain Zlotkowski."

"Zee, Frank Wilcox here, it's an immediate go. But, Zee, you only have about a five hour window to reach the site and return."

"With our flight time that will leave us enough time to do a good search, Colonel."

Wilcox was quiet for a moment and then said, "Zee, if the weather starts to turn bad you're to abort the mission. Do you understand me?"

Zlotkowski immediately replied, "Roger that, Colonel Wilcox. I think we'll be okay with a five hour window, and I'll not risk the safety of my crew, sir."

As Colonel Frank Wilcox hung up the phone, he wondered if his order to abort with bad weather just signed death certificates for Jim and David Wade, but he knew he had to think of the safety of his aircrews first. He stood, looked out his window for a moment and thought, Please, God, let my men find something.

An hour later the Colonel was in the command post listening to Save One, Zlotkowski's helicopter, as they neared the location where the commercial pilot had picked up the emergency beeper.

"Rescue Center, this is Save One and we are at the beeper location. I have nothing visual to report at this time. We have started our search pattern and I will keep you informed."

"Roger, Save One, understand you have started your search pattern."

Many long and tense minutes passed as Frank Wilcox sipped his cold coffee and waited to hear the radio come alive once more.

Finally Zee's voice said, "Center, Save One, we are picking up a very weak beacon on guard. We will move around a little and see if it will come in stronger."

"Roger, Save One, copy."

"Center," The radio broke the silence of the room a few minutes later, "we are where the signal is the strongest, but have nothing visual at, ah. . . wait one."

"I think they just saw something." The staff Sergeant seated at the radio said as he turned to look at the Colonel.

"Thank God, let's hope so, son." Wilcox spoke as he moved closer to the radio.

"Center, this is Save One, we have found the crash site. I repeat, we have found the crash site, but no sign of survivors. I'm sending a P.J. down to check the scene."

"Copy, you have the crash site visual. Keep us informed."

In the air, Captain Zlotkowski grew apprehensive as he realized there were no survivors on the ground near the crash. He'd been in the business long enough to know any survivors would be jumping and screaming like crazy people at the hovering aircraft. Looking back over his shoulder he asked, "John, you ready to go down?"

Sergeant John Banks was a United States Air Force Pararescue man, or P.J. as they were commonly called, and had long months of training behind him, as well as two years of active flying. While this was not his first rescue, it would be the first one with fatalities and it looked as if there were no survivors. He gave Zlotkowski a big grin and said, "Yes sir. I'll check the wreckage first and then contact you to let you know what I find."

The crew chief moved the forest penetrator over to where Banks could sit on the device as a winch lowered it. Once on the ground he would disconnect from the penetrator and then search for survivors. The P.J. positioned the device between his legs, disconnected his communications cable to the aircraft, and moved toward the open door. Stopping, he double-checked the strap from the device that ran under his arms and around his back. He then stepped out into space and the crew chief lowered him by winch to the snow.

The crew watched as Banks landed on the snow covered ground, disconnected from the forest penetrator, and slowly made his way to the crashed aircraft. Many long and tense minutes passed before Zlotkowski heard the young Sergeant say over the radio, "I've got one fatality in the pilot's seat. He appears to be a male of approximately thirty to forty years old with severe trauma to his head. There are signs of the kid, because the doctor's head is covered and the inside of the aircraft has been searched well. Do you want me to move out a bit and look for him?"

"Affirmative, Angel One, take a look around. In the mean time I'm going to pull up a bit and get out of this wind."

"Copy Save One, understand you're going up. I'll contact you when I find the boy. Angel One out."

"Center, this is Save One, we have a PJ on the ground and he has confirmed one fatality and it's Doctor Wade. Repeat, the doctor did not make it. He's found signs of a survivor, and he is looking for him now. The survivor must be David Wade. I repeat, Doctor Wade did not make it, but there is one survivor on the ground. Please confirm the tail numbers of Wade's aircraft, Oscar, Charlie, one, six, three, niner, seven."

"Roger on the tail number, Save One. Oscar, Charlie, one, six, three, niner, seven," Center replied a few seconds later.

Colonel Wilcox took the news of James Wade's death like a blow to the pit of his stomach. He sat down next to the Sergeant, closed his eyes and said in a low voice, "Please God, let David be alright."

The Sergeant beside him quickly turned and asked, "What was that, sir?"

"Nothing Sergeant, just a little prayer is all. There is a young boy on the ground alone and I hope we get to him in time."

"Save one, Angel One." Sergeant Banks radioed ten minutes later.

"Go Angel One." Zlotkowski quickly replied.

"I have found signs the boy survived the crash without serious injury, but it's confusing to say the least. I have a burnt up shelter, a big piece of melted plastic, a moose carcass, and some other signs that he has been in the area. I have not found the missing boy yet."

"Roger, I understand you have signs of the boy surviving but you have not located him yet. Is that correct Angel One?"

"Affirmative, Save One, the survivor has not been located as of this time."

Zlotkowski spoke into his mic as he moved around to get more comfortable in his seat, "Center, Save One, we have found signs the passenger of the plane survived. Angel One is still on the ground searching for him now. Our Poppa Juliet sees no evidence the boy is injured."

"Copy Save One, understand you have found signs of a young survivor, keep us posted."

Wilcox glanced at his watch and hoped the P.J. would find David Wade before he had to call off the mission. He was nearing the end of his mission window for the rescue and it would break his heart to have to call the crew home without the boy.

"Colonel Wilcox, weather is on line one for you, sir." A young female Airman First Class announced from her console.

Frank picked up the phone and punched the lit up button on the phone, "Colonel Wilcox."

"Colonel, Captain Johnston here. We are going to have to close your window a little early. Another front has developed and will hit within the hour. It developed suddenly over Russia and looks to be another huge blizzard headed our way. I'm sorry, sir."

Colonel Wilcox groaned, hung up the phone, and turned to the Sergeant at the radio console as he said, "Inform Save One, to remove the doctors body and return to base. We have a bad front due to hit in about an hour." The Colonel knew if the crew left now the flight would be close and after spending time to remove Jim's body, they would have to fly part of the return in a blizzard. Only, he didn't want them to return to base empty handed.

The orders were relayed to the helicopter and a few minutes of silence filled the room until finally they all heard, "Say again, Center."

"You are to remove the fatality and return to base immediately. Copy, Save One?"

"Uh, Copy Center, we are to remove the fatality and return to base." As Captain Zlotkowski spoke, he slowly shook his head. He knew if he flew away the young boy would surely die, but he also knew he couldn't disobey a lawful order without good cause. Finally, he spoke once more, "Angel One, remove the fatality. I repeat, remove the fatality and wait for further orders."

"But, Zee, I think the boy is close by."

"John, we're to remove the doctor's body and return to base."

"Roger, copy."

Ten minutes later the doctor's body was aboard the aircraft and covered with a wool blanket. The P.J. was still on the ground and as the penetrator lowered to him, he spoke, "Save One, request permission to stay on the ground and continue my search."

Zlotkowski knew how the young Sergeant felt, because he felt the same way, but as the aircraft commander, he couldn't allow it, regardless of what he might have wanted to do. "Denied, Angel One. Get on your ride, and let's call it a day."

"Zee, that kid is still out here and he's alive. He'll die if we leave him, and you know it, too!"

The young Captain felt his heart saying one thing and his head another, but he had his orders from his boss, "Angel One, you *will* get on the forest penetrator and come back on-board this aircraft. And, you will do it **now**."

Large flakes of snow had started falling and the wind had gotten worse just within the last few minutes.

Finally, the P.J. replied, "Copy Save One. I will be aboard in a few minutes."

Sergeant Banks was deeply upset. As a P.J. he'd been trained to save people, not leave them. He was torn between his training and his responsibilities to obey all lawful orders, but he knew without authorization he could not stay behind. Just as he was strapping himself into the forest penetrator he heard Zee voice over his radio, "Wait one, Angel One, I'll check with Center and see if they'll authorize you to stay behind."

"Rescue Center, Save One, I have a request from Angel One to remain on the ground. Do you copy?"

Wilcox heard the request and for many long minutes he battled the decision over and over in his head. He knew the P.J. was highly trained in survival and he'd still be alive when the weather broke. *Maybe, just maybe,* he thought, *he'll find David and keep him alive as well.* Finally, he simply nodded at the radio operator at the console.

"Save One, Rescue Center, be advised Angel One can remain on the ground. I repeat, your request is granted. Please acknowledge, Save One."

Zee gave a big smile and said, "Understand, Angel One is to stay on the ground."

The copilot looked over at Zlotkowski and said, "We need to drop him a survival kit."

Zee nodded and then said, "Angel One, you have permission to continue your search. Be advised it might be a while before we are in this area again. We are lowering a MA-1 survival kit at this time."

Banks gave a big grin and replied, "Roger that, Save One, I am to remain behind. Drop the kit."

Three minutes later, the survival kit was on the ground and Sergeant John Banks quickly moved it to the side, away from the blast of the chopper's blades.

He keyed his radio and said, "I've got the kit. When y'all get back this way again, drop in for a cup of hot coffee."

Zee laughed and replied, "Will do, Angel One, and my crew and I want to thank you for flying with treetop airlines. John, you take care, and we'll be back as soon as this weather breaks."

Sergeant Banks stood on the side of the mountain and watched Save One fly off. He watched until he could no longer see the rescue chopper. Then, he pulled the survival kit under some trees and starting constructing a shelter, because he knew it would grow very cold before long.

After waiting for the chopper to land, Colonel Frank Wilcox walked slowly to the aircraft as soon as the blades of the chopper stopped rotating. An ambulance was there to take James Wade's body away, but first Frank had to make sure the man aboard the aircraft was his friend. The old Colonel jumped up through the open side doors of the Huey UH-1, knelt by the body, and pulled the blanket back at the head. He immediately looked into the unseeing eyes of Doctor James Wade.

He was still shaking his head as he drove from the flight line and called his office, "Sergeant Sidwell, call Pastor Lucas at his home and tell him I'll pick him up in twenty minutes. Let the man know we found the crash site. Also, tell him I will give him more information when I see him."

About twenty-five minutes later, as Frank drove to Cathy Wades home, he filled the pastor in on what they'd found at the crash site. Finally, Pastor Lucas said, "Frank, do you think that Sergeant of yours will find David?"

"If Dave stuck around the crash site I'm sure Banks has found him already. But, pastor, if the boy has tried to walk out, well, we'll never find him."

"What do you think David would do? You've been in the woods with him many times."

Frank thought for a minute or so and then said, "It depends. I think David would stay there, unless he had a good reason to leave. He's a smart kid, Pastor, but we have to remember he is alone and most likely a pretty scared boy right now."

Too soon, as far as Frank was concerned they were at the Wade home. He and the pastor walked to the door and rang the doorbell. A minute or two later Cathy Wade opened the door.

As soon as she saw the pastor with Frank, she knew the news was not good. She lowered her head and said, "Please come in. I suspect you have some bad news for me, don't you, Frank?"

Colonel Wilcox didn't answer her until they were sitting on the sofa and then he turned to her and said softly, "Cathy, we found the crash site. Jim didn't make it, and we found him strapped in his seat. However, we found evidence David survived the crash, and I have a man on the ground looking for him as we speak."

Cathy closed her eyes, and Frank could see the tears running down her cheeks. She gave a low moan, her body quivered, and she used the back of her hand to wipe her eyes. Turning to Frank she asked, "W. . . when will we know about David?"

Frank realized she wouldn't want to hear what he was about to say, but he told her what he knew, "Sergeant Banks, the man on the ground, can only communicate with aircraft flying in the local area. His radio doesn't have the range to reach Elmendorf. So, as soon as the weather breaks we'll be back out. But, Cathy, we will go back and as soon as we can.

Remember, our P.J. found sign that David is alive, so all we can do now is wait until he's found."

"T. . . thank you. . . Frank. I know you'll do what you can. Now, if you'll both excuse me, I want to be alone. Marie will be home from school soon, and I have to prepare myself to tell her what has happened."

"Cathy, I can stay with you, if you wish," Pastor Lucas said with a sad smile.

"I. . .I think I'd like that."

Frank stood, slowly shook his tired head, and left the house. He knew the death of Jim would be hard on Cathy as well as Marie, but he also knew from years in search and rescue that not all recoveries turned out well. Frank realized he would miss Jim very much, but any time a person strapped an airplane to their rump things could go wrong. Some people would think Colonel Frank Wilcox was a hard man without feelings, but as he drove home, tears slowly started falling from his eyes. He knew death, and he knew it well from years at his job, but the death of a close friend always hurt him most.

Frank had no more than entered the house when Carol saw his face and asked, "They got to the crash site?"

"Yes, Carol, and Jim was killed. We have some signs that David survived, and I have a man on location looking for him."

"Has Cathy been told yet?"

"Pastor Lucas and I told her a few minutes ago. You know, Carol, there are times, like this, when I hate my job."

Carol moved closer to her husband and pulled him to her as she said, "Frank, you climb up out of your pity-pot and you do it right now. You and your men have thousands of saves under your belts and we both know you can't save all of them."

Frank gave his wife a dry smile and replied, "I know honey, but I hated telling Cathy that Jim was dead. It tore my heart out to see what my words did to her."

"Frank, is she still alone?"

"No, Pastor Lucas is with her. He will be with her when she tells Marie what has happened. I just hope my P.J. finds David safe and sound."

"Right now I want you to take a long hot shower, eat, and then relax a little. There is nothin' more you can do right now, except clean up, and get some rest. If you get a call, I'll let you know. Later on tonight, I'm going over to spend the night with Cathy. She shouldn't be alone on a night like this, Frank."

Frank showered, ate, and afterward called the weather shop, "Colonel Wilcox here, can you tell me how long this new front will last?"

"Sure, Colonel," A young Airman said over the phone, "it looks like it might blow over in about three days. If it starts to break earlier do you want us to call you?"

"Sure, son, call me the minute you have an open window in the weather."

"Will do, sir, and I'll put it in the log book so all of the weather guys know to give you a call. You have a good evening, Colonel and call anytime you need an update."

Frank hung up the phone, poured a cup of hot coffee and moved to the sofa. He'd try to read an hour or two and then get some sleep. Carol had already left for the Wade home, so he'd have a long night alone. After serving in rescue during both Vietnam and Operation Desert Storm, he'd always hated being alone following a bad mission. No, he didn't have bad dreams or feel afraid; he just liked to be around other people after things had turned ugly. And, as far as

Colonel Frank Wilcox was concerned, this day had been one of his worst days.

CHAPTER 10

Search as he might, Sergeant Banks had found no other signs of David, and he suspected the falling snow had covered his tracks. He discovered the burnt shelter, as well as the shelter under the pine tree, and other indicators the young man had killed a moose, but it was as if David Wade had walked off the face of the earth. Finally, darkness forced the P.J. to seek shelter from the high winds and blowing snow. He decided to continue his search in the morning, if the weather would only cooperated a little.

At six that evening, Banks pulled his pocket thermometer out and saw it was twenty degrees below zero. He realized that David had to have a good shelter constructed, a fire, and dry clothes or he was dead. But, since he'd survived up to this point alone, the P.J. figured young David knew what to do and could do it. When he had searched the area earlier he'd looked for some sign that Dave had been injured, but he'd found nothing. Usually he would have found some bloody cloth, blood in a shelter, or even discarded bandages, but there had been nothing. What he'd found also told the P.J. a lot about the young boy he was looking for. It seemed that David Wade was not seriously injured, woods smart, and a very intelligent young man. *All of those things he'll need, if we're to find him alive,* John Banks thought as he added wood to his small fire.

The log had no sooner fell into the dancing flames when he heard a low growl from the darkness near the carcass of the dead moose. *Bear!* Banks thought, *But, is it a black or grizzly? Lord, don't make it a grizzly, I don't even have a weapon.*

Thinking quickly, the P.J. pulled out his Mark 13 Mod 0 day/night flare, removed the plastic cover over the night end and allowed the o-ring on a cord to dangle freely. He knew once the flare fired by pulling the o-ring, it would ignite with nearly a million-candle power, and his only hope was the bright light would scare the bear away if it came too near.

From out of the darkness came a huge black mass. It stood, unthreatening, until the flickering flames of the fire allowed Banks to see a fully-grown grizzly bear. The bear, standing on its hind legs, was way over a thousand pounds, and was more than seven feet tall. As a knot of fear formed in his stomach, the P.J. grasped the o-ring in his right hand and thought, *if he moves much closer, I'll have to pull the ring.*

The bear abruptly dropped to all fours and charged at Banks, stopping only about six feet away breathing hard. As his hands trembled, the man pulled the o-ring on the flare and immediately a bright light spewed from the end of the canister. Turing his head to avoid injuries to his eyes from the burning magnesium and to prevent night blindness, Banks heard the hiss of the flare as it burned and then a loud grunt of surprise from the bear. Glancing at movement across his fire, he saw the bear making his way at a wild run toward the protective cover of the trees. His flare had just saved his life.

Banks added more wood to his fire, gave a short prayer of thanks, and leaned back on his sleeping bag. The bear had given a false charge and most likely was unsure what Banks had been. If he'd taken Banks for prey the charge would have continued. The P.J. knew a little about bear attacks and it was the first one he'd had to face, but he decided he didn't like it at all. *There is something frightening about a beast that size charging a man,* he thought as he placed another flare beside his hand for easy reach.

The remainder of the night was quiet, though Banks slept poorly and half expected the bear to return. He awoke with his neck stiff and his stomach empty. Snow was still falling, but not as hard as when he'd been forced to call off his search. Kneeling by his fire pit, he found a live ember in the ash and soon had a fire started. Opening an MRE he discovered to his delight he had a ham slice, rice, pound cake, cheese spread, powdered cocoa and some other odds and ends. He placed the sealed pouch containing the ham and rice into a large pot of boiling water and ten minutes later, he was eating his breakfast. The meal would provide him with around 1300 calories, more than enough to help keep him warm as he searched for David. He placed the gum and other small items from the accessory packet in his right cargo pocket of his battle dress uniform.

The sky was a dark gray and the wind was slight as Banks moved from his shelter and made his way up the animal trail to the top of the mountain. He moved slowly to avoid overheating and guessed the temperature to be near ten below zero. During the winter months and with bad weather, he would have less than four hours to search before darkness came. At the top, he pulled out a small pair of binoculars and scanned the open tundra below the mountain. At first, he saw nothing, but then he spotted something moving. He adjusted his binoculars and the distance was just too far off to make out any details. All Banks was able to see was a solitary figure and it appeared to be human in form. As he looked the areas over closely, he spotted a thin line of smoke near the horizon coming from a group of trees.

I think that's you, David Wade, and you're headed toward the smoke. You must think it's a trapper or a group of Natives and it might well be, Banks thought as he placed his binoculars back in his parka.

Returning to his shelter, Sergeant Banks quickly packed his gear, put out his fire, and started down the mountainside. He'd already combed the crash site and David wasn't there, so the lone figure out on the tundra must be the young man. *He's a smart lad,* Banks thought while stepping over a log on the trail, *he spotted that smoke too and knew it might be his only means of surviving.*

Nearing the bottom of the mountain near dark, Banks quickly constructed a snow trench, lined it with his sleeping mat and covered it with snow blocks. Climbing inside his shelter, he used his backpack as a door. He quickly cut a vent hole in the roof to allow airflow and thought, *Tomorrow I need to get rid of some gear. My pack must weigh over sixty pounds and I can't carry that much over the open tundra. I need to move quickly and I'll not be able to do it with this load.*

An hour later, Banks removed his pack from the shelter opening, stuck his head out and saw it was snowing hard. He left the entrance open and pulled out a small stove that burned compressed fuel blocks about the size of a sugar cube. He placed a cube on his folding stove, placed a canteen cup on top, and heated some water from his canteen to make a cup of cocoa. As the water heated, he hoped David had enough sense to seek shelter in a hard snowfall and suspected the young man did.

Sergeant Banks knew then David would have stayed at the crash site and close to his father's body, except he'd seen the distant smoke as well. It was obvious that some sort of people lived where the smoke was at, but what would he find? If it was an old trapper, he might have a snow machine, a dog team, or perhaps nothing more than snowshoes. If it was a Native village, it might even have a radio so he could communicate with Elmendorf Air Force Base. If not, then David and Banks would have to wait until Save One returned and then contact them with the PRC-90 survival radio. It wouldn't have great range, but if Banks could see the chopper he should be able to talk to it, unless his batteries died between now and the rescue attempt.

As he sipped his hot cocoa, he opened another MRE and smiled when he realized it was one of his favorites, Grilled Chicken with Mexican Rice. The side dishes and accessories were pretty much the same he'd had with the earlier meal, except instead of cocoa he now had a small package of coffee. He decided to eat the pound cake as dessert and then get some sleep. *Tomorrow, if the weather will allow, I'll make a fast trek over the tundra toward the smoke, he thought as he lowered the food pouch into the canteen cup of hot water.*

Later, his meal finished, Banks stuck his feet inside his sleeping bag, pulled out a small pocket tablet and made some entries of what had happened so far. His notes served two purposes as far as he was concerned; if he should die the notes would explain his actions and thoughts during the rescue attempt, and if he lived, the notes would help him write up his post rescue report. Not to mention it would make his debriefing much easier with the notes to jog his memory. Finishing his notes, Banks rolled up his parka to use as a pillow, crawled down inside his sleeping bag and called it a day.

Near sunrise the next morning, Banks was going through his backpack. Making two piles, he placed the items to leave in one and items to take in another. He kept his medical gear, individual survival kit, and some personal items that he'd picked up during his career. His survival knife, signaling equipment, and spare socks he placed in the pile to keep. The survival manual, excess MRE's, cans of water, and other not need items he discarded. But, before he set the MRE's aside, he pulled the coffee and cocoa packets as well as the candies or sugars. He'd keep the drinks to stay warm and the candies and sugars for energy. By the time he'd gone through his pack he'd lost about half of his load, but then he went through it all again and removed more unneeded gear. His survival kit, the one dropped by Save 1, was designed for people to stay in place and not move, so it was heavy, designed for large groups, and most of the equipment wasn't need when traveling. He went through it again and left a larger pile near the entrance.

The sun was just making its way through the gray clouds when Banks left his shelter and started across the tundra with a much lighter pack. He pulled the flaps down on his "mad bomber" hat and wrapped a scarf over his nose and mouth. It was bone freezing cold and if the wind picked up, he'd have to find shelter. The wind caused loose snow to whirl around and around like small white dust devils.

* * *

David, less than two miles in front of Sergeant Banks, was very cold and knew he'd have to find shelter shortly if the wind didn't die down. He suspected it was forty below with the wind chill and he was already shaking. He'd eaten the last of his meat, what little the wolves had left him, the night before and only had hot water for breakfast. He'd spent a cold night in his shelter and more than once woke shivering from the intense cold, but he'd survived. When he checked his feet this morning he noticed the cracked skin under his toe was better, but he'd have to watch it closely to avoid frostbite. His father had once told him that injured body parts were more susceptible to cold related injuries than healthy ones. The last thing David wanted or needed while walking to safety was to have his feet go bad on him. *Bad feet or hands will get me killed,* he thought as he pulled the casualty blanket around his shoulders tighter.

He had a headache and noticed his vision appeared to be blurred, but he suspected it was from the wind. As he struggled through the deep snow, it dawned on him that he was in serious trouble. Someone had explained the symptoms of hypothermia to him once, it may have been in school, and he realized he had the injury. I've got to get out of the cold and warm up, he thought as he came to a stop and started digging in the snow. In just a few minutes, he had another snow trench constructed and as he crawled inside, he remembered to make a ventilation hole too.

As the small twigs and sticks he'd collected on his crude sled burned near the mouth of his shelter, he tried to remember what he could about hypothermia. He knew it was the lowering of the body's core temperature and it killed in little time. The treatment, if he remembered correctly, was to warm up from the inside and keep his outside warm, as well as dry, at the same time. He wrapped the casualty blanket around his body tightly and then made a cup of hot water. As he sipped the water, he could feel his body heat returning. *I came close to dying a few minutes ago. I have to start paying attention or this weather will kill me,* he thought as he raised his cup to his lips.

Once the water was finished, David fell asleep. Never in his young life had he ever been so tired, sleepy and hungry.

Banks discovered David's tracks in the snow quickly once back on the trail and realized the young man was near. Sergeant Banks was wearing aluminum-framed snowshoes, but he could see where the survivor had sunk in the snow up to his knees as he moved. *I've got to find this guy quickly; because walking in this snow will either fatigue him to the point he'll get hypothermia, or he'll just lie down and go to sleep. In either case, this weather will kill him,* the P.J. thought as he noticed the tracks were more uneven now and it was obvious David was exhausted.

As he followed the tracks, Banks noticed David no longer walked in a straight line but meandered all over the tundra. *He's come down with hypothermia,* the P.J. thought, *I hope he knows the symptoms, or I'll find him dead.*

The wind shifted and increased in strength from the north. Banks stopped, pulled his face mask off and sniffed the air. *Smoke,* he thought, *and it's from the north. It looks like David has at least a shelter and fire.*

Lowering his face mask, Banks began a fast walk toward the smoke he'd smelled. The wind was blistering cold now and the air filled with blowing snow, which stung his eyes, so he removed his goggles from his coat and put them on. With the wind as high as it was, he knew he'd never see the smoke and there was a good chance he'd walk right by David's shelter. Slowing, he began to search the snow around the tracks looking for some indication of a shelter or fire. While he moved slowly, his eyes were quickly scanning every inch, hoping to spot the survivor.

After almost a half an hour, Banks noticed metal in the snow off to his right. The wind was so high he no longer could see David's tracks, and he suspected they'd been filled in by blowing snow. He leaned over and walked into the wind to the metal. Kneeling, he raised the metal sheet and immediately saw a snow trench. *Lord, I hope it's David, or I'll never find him in this weather,* Banks thought as he called out in a loud voice, "David, are you in there?"

It took the young man a few seconds to clear his mind of sleep. Although he was unsure if he'd really heard his named called, he replied, "Yes, it's me, and I'm freezing!"

"David, I'm going to enlarge your shelter, so I can get in with you. I will dig another trench beside yours and the last thing I will do is cave the wall in between the two trenches. Once I'm finished I'll fix you some hot food, get you a drink, and warm you up. Are you able to understand me David?"

"Y. . . yes, I understand and I'll wait." David replied weakly.

Banks lowered his backpack onto the entrance to the young man's shelter, to help block the wind, pulled his folding shovel and started digging a trench. Once the snow was removed, he knocked the wall down to David's shelter, placed a casualty blanket on top of his trench, and held it in place by using snow blocks. As soon as the shelter was in good shape, he crawled inside, made another ventilation hole near the edge of the casualty blanket and started a fire with his portable stove. As the water heated for a cup of cocoa, he gave David a quick looking over.

After a minute or two Banks said, "David, you came really close to having hypothermia, and I see some white patches of damaged tissue on your face, ears and right hand. We'll warm you up real good first and then treat the tissue problem."

"I'm glad you found me! Who are you and how'd you get here."

Sergeant Banks explained who he was, all that had happened, and then said, "We'll get you back in good physical condition and then continue on to the smoke we saw. First, have a couple of hot drinks, eat an MRE, and get some rest. After all of that, I'll look at the damaged tissue again and see if we need to thaw it out or wrap it."

"Sergeant Banks, thank you for coming for me and my dad." As David spoke, Banks could hear the sorrow in his voice.

"David, just call me John. I'm a pararescue man and it's my job in the Air Force to rescue people. I'm sorry about the loss of your father, but I'm glad you made it. Too many times all we find is a crashed plane and no survivors."

"My father was in the Air Force once and he taught survival."

"I know, Colonel Wilcox told me all about your father, and you. I think it was your father's training that kept you alive, wasn't it?"

David lowered his eyes and replied, "Uh-huh, he taught me things in ways I didn't know I was being taught. Usually he just had me do things and I'd learn as I went along. He was always telling me stories, jokes, and different things about the outdoors."

Seeing the young man was exhausted, Banks placed his right hand on David's shoulder and said, "Get some hot food in you now and then use my sleeping bag. You'll find it very warm compared to the casualty blanket you've been using."

David had two hot drinks, ate a meal, and fell asleep in the sleeping bag with a smile on his face.

CHAPTER 11

The snow in Anchorage was up to the bumper on Colonel Wilcox's truck, and it was still snowing, as he opened the door. He glanced around and noticed very little traffic on the base, which meant the Base Commander had shut the place down due to weather. The weather guessers were calling for more snow off and on overnight, with an additional six inches by morning. Entering the truck and closing the door, he started the engine and waited for the heater to defrost the inside of his windshield. The outside of the windshield he'd scraped clean a few minutes earlier.

The handheld radio, commonly referred to as 'the brick' by military personnel, sudden came on and he heard a voice say, "SAR One, this is the command post."

Pushing the transmit button, Wilcox replied, "Command post, go."

"Sir, the weather continues to worsen, but the weather forecasters asked me to notify you that they see a clearing coming in about forty-eight hours."

"Are they pretty sure of the time line?"

"The officer in charge said it should happen in about two days, but he was unsure how long it would last."

"Roger, keep me informed of the weather and check with the honor guard to see if the Wade family has requested an escort with the aircraft returning Doctor Wade's remains to New Mexico."

"I'll check, sir, and let you know."

As he laid the brick down on the seat of his truck, Wilcox wondered what Cathy would do. He'd suggested she not take Jim's body back for burial until David was found, but she'd not answered him. *Most likely,* he thought as he pulled from the parking lot, *she's still in shock.*

Carol was not home, so after a hot shower, dinner, and a little television, he called Cathy, "Cathy, is my wife over there?"

"Yes, do you want to speak with her?"

"No, it's okay. I was just wondering where she disappeared to, is all."

"Frank, I want to thank you and Carol for the support you've given me the last week. I have had a pretty rough time of it, but you've both helped me so much."

"You are a friend in need, Cathy, and I'm doing just what you'd do if our situations were reversed. Don't hesitate to ask if we can help you in any way at all."

"T . . . thank you."

"Cathy, I hate to bring this up, but shouldn't you hold off taking Jim to New Mexico until the weather clears enough for us to look for David?"

A few seconds of silence followed, but finally she replied, "I've given that some additional thought and decided to wait. I guess at first I thought Dave was dead as well, but I'm beginning to think he might survive this. He'll want to be there when his father is buried."

"Sergeant Banks, he's the P.J. on the ground, is one of the best men I have and if anyone can find David it'll be him. Remember, my men and I have dedicated our lives to saving others."

"Isn't your motto, 'That others may live'?"

"Yep, it is, and the pararescue creed says it best, 'It is my duty as a Pararescueman to save a life and to aid the injured. I will perform my assigned duties quickly and efficiently, placing these duties before personal desires and comforts. These things I do, that others may live.' And it's a pretty serious bunch of words to us, with a heck of a lot of meaning."

"Frank, I know you and your men are doing your best and I find myself having highs and lows as I worry about David. I know all of you are dedicated to saving him, only I really don't know how much more of this I can take."

"Cathy, my job is never easy and the hardest part is the waiting and telling people bad news. When I was in Vietnam and the Gulf War it was different, and someone back in the states did the notifying of the next of kin. All I did was drive a Jolly Green Giant helicopter so my pararescue teams had a platform to work from as they did their jobs. But, since I've become the commander of this organization it's my responsibility to do a lot of things I didn't have to do as a young Captain. Right now, the best thing you can do is what you suggested last night."

Silence followed and then Cathy asked, "What was that? I'm sorry, Frank, but I don't remember."

"You spoke of having some family members come up here to spend some time with you. You were considering Jim's parents as well as your own. I personally think that's a great idea. It's not good for you and Marie to be alone right now, not after all that has happened. You need good solid family support for a while and they'll do wonders for your emotions."

"I remember now. I just had so many different thoughts going through my head the last few days that I can't remember what I had for lunch."

Frank chuckled and replied, "I can and it wasn't much. A bag of chips, a cola, and a candy bar."

"Frank, I have to go and start dinner. Would you like to come over and eat with us?"

"No, I just ate, but I'll take a cup of coffee if you have some."

"I'll put a pot on and tell Carol you're on your way over. Frank, thanks again, because the two of you have been true friends."

"Get the coffee on, I'll be right over."

* * *

At five O'clock the next morning, Colonel Wilcox was at his desk sorting through a large pile of rescue messages from all over the world. There had been a private plane crash in California, an American ship taking on water in the China Sea, and a commercial airliner had gone down in South America with no survivors. Then there were the update messages from previously reported rescue efforts. He sipped his coffee, shook his head, and realized that in most of these cases, there were no survivors. What did please him was that when there were survivors, search and rescue had not lost a single person. That told him his chosen profession was made up of highly trained professionals who took their jobs seriously.

His phone rang and he picked it up, "Colonel Wilcox speaking."

"Frank, it's General Moores, you got a minute?"

Wilcox laughed and thought, *now who wouldn't have a minute if a General officer wanted to talk to them?* But he replied, "I'll be right there, sir."

Entering the General's office, Colonel Wilcox walked up to the man's desk, stopped at about four feet and saluted as he said, "Colonel Frank Wilcox reporting as ordered sir."

The General returned his salute and said, "Have a seat, Frank, and let's keep this informal today."

"Yes sir, as you wish." Wilcox replied as he sat down in an overstuffed chair in front of the General's desk.

"Now, tell me what you know about Doctor Wade's son, David isn't it?"

"Not much I can tell you other than what I wrote in my earlier report sir."

"Frank, I'm well aware of what the report said, but I want to know about this P.J. and whether he's found the boy yet."

"Our last contact with Save One was when the P.J. requested to stay behind. We've had no other contact since then but it is safe to bet that Banks, the P.J., is doing fine. We have no way of knowing if he's found David or not."

"I've thought of that. The only radio your man on the ground would have is the PRC-90, which has extremely short range, correct?"

"Yes sir, the radio is designed for line of sight use and there is no way he can contact Elmendorf."

The General chuckled and said, "I know the radio very well. In Vietnam I spent three days hiding in the jungle from the communists and that little radio was my only hope of rescue."

"The problem we have is the weather. If the weather doesn't clear soon the batteries in the radio Banks has might die, due to cold."

The General leaned back in his chair, closed his eyes, and then said, "A radio in a non-combat rescue is just a luxury. Since no one will be shooting at us, it's likely Banks will have signals out, and I've seen some good ones in my time. He still has his smoke flares, his pen-gun flares, signal mirror and signal panel. He'll be able to contact us when we arrive, as long as he's healthy and in good shape."

"I just meant the radio would speed the rescue up sir, especially if Banks has had to leave the crash site."

"Why in the world would he do that? We're all trained to stay near the crash site, so I don't see your P.J. wondering off."

"Sir, Banks reported he had not found the survivor on the ground and a man like him will do whatever it takes to find David."

"So, you think this Wade boy would walk off that mountain?"

Colonel Wilcox thought for a minute and then replied, "No, not unless he had a good reason. If something forced him to move, then he'd move, but I don't think that, under normal circumstances, the boy would leave the aircraft wreckage."

"What makes you so confident in this kid's abilities and thinking, Frank?"

"I know him very well and his father was one of the best when he taught survival. I'm confident we'll find David near the crash site or someplace safe and sound. I just don't see him walking off that mountain for no reason. Besides, I don't think he'd want to leave his father's body."

"When the high winds drop, and what I mean is at any time you have a safe window to fly, you get a bird over the crash site and try to contact Sergeant Banks."

"Yes sir, I'll do that. If Banks is safe he'll come on the radio at fifteen minutes after and prior to each hour, just to monitor the frequency."

The General chuckled once more and said, "Uh-huh, I remember the radio routine well. I can assure you, when you do contact him that first message you send will make his day."

"Will there be anything else sir?" Colonel Wilcox started to stand.

"Sit back down Frank and let's discuss Sergeant Banks for a moment. Now, you know I don't just give medals away and I'm a firm believer the recipient has to earn each of them, but Banks will deserve something once this is all over. Perhaps even a promotion."

Wilcox nodded and said, "Sir, I think he'd be pleased with whatever medal you pin on his shirt. He's not in his job for medals."

"Well, you give the medal some serious thought and let me know later which ones you've decided to submit him for. I'll not hesitate to endorse it, because any man who'll spend days out in minus twenty-degree weather looking for a survivor surely deserves to be recognized officially. And, you make sure his next performance report is routed though this office, I've some good things to say about Sergeant John Banks."

"I'll do that sir, in both cases."

"That's it, Frank. Keep on top of the weather and keep it safe."

Colonel Wilcox stood, saluted the General, and quickly left the office. Once back in his office he called the weather station, got an update, and then notified Zlotkowski and Baldwin of the mission to fly over the crash site.

He heard Zee's voice on the phone reply, "Roger that sir, as soon as we have a clear window we'll leave. I'll keep it safe too sir, just keep me informed of the weather so I don't get trapped out there."

"Zee, just do your best and I'll be satisfied."

"Will do, sir."

"Take care and good luck." Colonel Wilcox said as he hung the phone up.

Picking the phone up, the colonel called the life support shop and heard a voice answer, "Life support, Sergeant Hopkins speaking, may I help you?"

"Sergeant Hopkins, this is Colonel Wilcox of SAR, can you tell me the battery life of a PRC-90 radio."

"Sure sir, it's usually six to eight hours, but high and low temperatures can affect that time zone. See, if it's too cold the battery may die for a period of time, but if the survivor warms it up it can be used again. We teach downed aircrews to keep the radio warm at all times, so they can use the radio when they need it."

"How many batteries come with the PRC-90?"

"That depends on which survival kit or gear it's packed, sir. In the MD-1 survival kit there isn't a spare, while the SRU-21/P survival vest has one spare. Of course the large life raft survival kits have two spares."

"Thanks Sergeant Hopkins, but one last question."

"Yes sir?"

"Do the P.J.'s get their survival equipment refresher training from you guys and gals at the life support shop?"

"No, sir, the P.J.'s have a life support technician detached to them."

Of course, the Colonel thought, *I knew that. The position just opened a few months back.* But, he said, "I appreciate your information, Sergeant."

"Not a problem, Colonel, and feel free to call us any time."

If the P.J.'s have their own life support section, I don't have to ask how well Banks does in training. Obviously, he's good or the instructor would have said something to me. I'm just surprised I forgot Airman Wilson and that's not good at all. It just goes to prove I'm too far removed the real action and missing a lot of information, Colonel Wilcox thought as he picked up his cup of coffee and took a sip.

"Sir, I hate to bother you, but there is a newspaper man out by my desk asking to speak to you." Technical Sergeant Malory said as he stuck his head in the doorway.

"A what?"

"A reporter, sir, and he said he wants to speak with you, about the Wade rescue."

"Keep him waiting until I clear this through public affairs." Colonel Wilcox replied as he picked up the phone once more.

"Major French, public affairs, how may I help you?"

"Major, Colonel Wilcox here, did you authorize a newspaper reporter to interview me today?"

"Uh, yes sir, but that was just a few minutes ago and I didn't have time to let you know."

"The next time you *will* call me first and coordinate all interviews, won't you, Major French? I dislike surprises, Major."

"I'm sorry sir, except I thought one of my people had already spoken with you."

"Well, they didn't." Wilcox closed the line and thought, *A newspaper reporter! This is not good at all. I'll have to be careful how I answer this man's questions or I'll be misquoted in print.*

Finishing his coffee, he called Sergeant Malory on the intercom and had the reporter sent in. The man was dressed in a military surplus parka, had snow boots on, and his mittens were hanging on cords tied to his sleeves. He was a young man, not over twenty-five, good looking, and his eyes spoke of a deep intelligence.

"Glad to see you, Colonel. My name is Williams, and I work for the Anchorage Daily Dispatch." The reporter spoke with a Midwestern twang.

"Have a seat, Mister Williams. Now, what can I do for you?" Colonel Wilcox said and pulled a pen from the top middle drawer of his desk.

115

"I have a few questions about the Wade crash."

"Okay, I'll answer them if I can."

"Would you say Doctor Wade was a good pilot? I ask this question because I understand you knew him personally."

"He was certified and qualified to fly and as far as I knew he was an excellent pilot."

"Does the Air Force have any idea of what caused the crash?"

Careful here, he's fishing for a reason for the crackup, the Colonel thought but said, "The United States Air Force is only assisting in the rescue efforts and the FAA will determine the cause of the crash, not us. The cause of the crash is actually a civilian matter."

"I understand." Williams replied as his pen moved on the small tablet he held on his right knee. And then, he asked, "Has there been any word of David Wade and the pararescueman left behind?"

I wonder where he found out about Banks, Wilcox thought. "At this time the weather has us socked in, and we've not been able to get airborne to continue the rescue. So, to answer your question, no, we've no word since the man was left behind to look for the lone survivor. By the way, Sergeant Banks requested to stay behind to continue his mission."

"Do you think you could arrange an interview with Doctor Wade's wife for me? I have a few questions I'd like to ask her." Williams asked and then gave a shy grin.

"I'll ask Cathy Wade, but I can make no promises." The Colonel replied quickly, knowing he'd not ask. She had enough on her plate without dealing with reporters.

"One last question sir, when will rescue efforts resume and how long will it take to get the two people out?"

"We cannot get into the air until this front passes. How long the actual rescue will take depends on a number of factors, such as wind, weather, where the rescue takes place, as well as the physical and mental condition of both people on the ground."

Standing, Willis said, "I think I have enough to do a story. I've interviewed some of Doctor Wade's friends, the FAA, the control tower, and of course, you. The tower folks didn't tell me much, except to say the crash was under investigation and they couldn't talk about it."

The next morning over breakfast, Colonel Wilcox almost choked on his coffee when he read the headlines, 'USAF Leaves a Man Behind During Rescue Attempt.' He felt his face turning red in anger and heard Carol ask, "What's the matter, Frank, you're as red as a beet."

Holding the paper so his wife could read the headlines, he said, "It makes it look like we left Banks behind by accident and that's not the way it happened at all!"

CHAPTER 12

F our hours later the storm was still blowing hard, but Banks had determined David's skin tissue was just a little frost nip and not anything serious. When the young man had awakened most of his normal color had returned to his face and hand, indicating all he needed was to warm up. Over a meal of MRE stew, the two talked of what was to come.

"I've only one pair of snowshoes, so the going will be slow. From what I could tell, we are less than three miles from where the smoke was," Banks spoke as he leaned back on his casualty blanket.

"We'll just have to go slowly then. I know with you along we'll get there, but I wasn't so sure when I was alone. I've never been as frightened in my life as I was when I realized my father was dead."

Banks gave the young man a weak grin and said, "That's to be expected. We grow up with our parents taking care of us and in a situation like the one you faced; your survival security disappeared with the death of your father. David, I know your father would be proud of you, because I am. Of all the environments in the world to survive in, the arctic cold and desert heat are the two extremes. But, you not only survived, you took actions to make sure you survived and that makes you different than most folks."

"Different? How so?"

The P.J. chuckled and replied, "Most folks simply live until they are rescued, but you did what needed to be done to insure you'd survive. Things like killing the moose, making a shelter, building a fire, making jerky, and the list goes on. You're different than many survivors, because your actions directly resulted in your survival."

"I just did what needed to be done, that's all. I have to admit though; I did some pretty stupid things at first."

Once again, Banks laughed and said, "It was your first time as a survivor, so it's expected. Not to mention you were facing the death of your father, extremely low temperatures, and your first night in the woods all alone. You did very well, all things considered."

"How will my mom be notified of dad's death?" David asked seriously.

"Colonel Wilcox and a priest or minister will go to your home to inform her. Then, if she wishes, the religious representative will stay with her so they can pray or talk. It's a terrible job, filled with lots of emotions, but the Colonel has been doing it for years. I suspect in your case he'll have a rough time of it, since he was a friend of your father."

David said, "I like the Colonel, and he's been a friend of the family as long as I can remember. I think he'll help my sister and mother as much as he can, but they'll be worried sick about me."

"There is nothing I can do right now and no way to let them know I've found you, either. We'll go to the smoke, stay there until the weather breaks, and then I'll signal a rescue aircraft. The Air Force knows I'm out here, so they'll be back. We try to never leave a person behind, even in combat situations."

Silence filled the small shelter until Banks reached into his backpack and removed a pair of wool socks.

Handing them to David he said, "Change your socks and put these on. They're made of wool and will keep your feet toasty warm even if they get wet. In the morning before we head out I have some other clothing items I want you to wear."

David removed his hiking boots, pulled off his old socks and was surprised at how comfortable the new wool socks were. His old socks were cotton and his feet had felt frozen as he'd walked. He knew immediately the wool would be much warmer, and he smiled as he felt his feet warming up.

The rest of the evening went by with the two making small talk, snacking on candy and sipping hot drinks. Finally, Banks and David went to sleep, with the young man in the sleeping bag and the P.J. in the casualty blanket. Just before he drifted off to sleep, Banks looked over at sleeping David Wade and said in a low voice, "Thank you, God."

Morning came with the air bone chilling cold and thick clouds overhead. Standing by the shelter, David was wearing a bright orange jacket that kept him warm, along with a facemask, mittens, and his wool socks. While Banks only had one pair of goggles, he gave them to the young man and smeared some soot from a candle under his eyes. David had lost the pair he'd started with, so he appreciated the eye protection. Banks knew the dark line under his eyes would protect him from snow blindness if the sun made even a token appearance. Turning to David he asked, "You ready to go? If the weather holds we should be at the smoke before noon."

Grinning, David replied, "Let's move then, I'd like to spend tonight in a cabin or a tent. I'm tired of sleeping in the snow and waking up half frozen each morning."

The two moved forward and the only sound was the crunching of the snow as David's feet broke though the frozen top layer. Banks had considered giving the snowshoes to the young man, but David admitted he'd never worn them before and they took some getting use to. The wind was light, no snow falling, and they both expected to be safe within a few hours.

Mile after cold mile was covered, with short breaks taken at times to avoid overheating and to give David a rest. Walking in deep snow is very difficult; only those in top physical shape can do it for very long. Finally, after two hours, they stopped for a quick hot drink and then got back on the trail.

Near noon, they saw a group of trees at the base of a mountain and David wanted to scream for joy!

Banks spoke as he looked at David and grinned, "We'll be at the trees in a few minutes and then we'll have to find the source of the smoke. I see a thin finger of smoke off to the left and we'll head that direction once we enter the woods. Keep a lookout for a hunting trail or dog trail leading in that direction. The odds are there are some trails leading to the open tundra, so all we have to do is find one and follow it back to the cabin."

Less than an hour later, the two stood in the falling snow looking at a rough trapper's cabin made of logs. Chained dogs were at a shed, a cache with long spider like legs was behind the cabin, and smoke was coming from a crooked stovepipe on the roof. The dogs began to bark loudly and suddenly the door to the cabin opened. An old man, holding a hunting rifle in his hands, walked out and looked around.

"Hello the cabin! I am Sergeant Banks of the United States Air Force and there's been an aircraft crash in the mountains."

"Airplane crash? I don't know nothin' 'bout no crash. Come on in and tell me what in tarnation is a-goin' on."

After being out in the cold for days, the heat in the small cabin overwhelmed Dave. The sides of the old woodstove in the corner were glowing red-hot as they entered. Placing his gun on a rack near the door, the old trapper turned and asked, "Now, would ya mind tellin' me what's goin' on?"

Banks explained what happened and then said, "The military will be out looking for me with the first break of good weather."

"Son, that might not be fer weeks yet. I've had the weather sock me in for long periods of time out here. My name is Thomas Brisk, but my friends all call me Vittles." The trapper replied.

David saw the trapper was a short man, maybe just a little over five feet tall, had gray hair and beard, and very alert eyes. He was dressed in wool clothing and wore snow boots, as well as a wolf skin hat with long earflaps on it. The flaps were tied up and at times the trapper would squint, as if he once wore glasses and was now forced to be without them.

"Vittles? How did you come to have a name like that?" David asked as he gave the man a smile.

"I eat a lot and just about anything I can get my hands on, too." Vittles replied with a low chuckle and then continued, "And, speaking of eating, I've got a big pot of stew on the stove. So ya both can eat a hot meal in a couple of hours. Right now, I want the both of ya to change into some dry clothes, have a cup of my coffee, and then get some sleep."

"I don't have any dry clothes." David said as he met the old trapper's eyes.

"Heck fire, son, ya can wear some of mine. I'm a short feller, so they'll fit ya I think. They might be large at the waist, but I've got some twine we can tie 'em up with. We'll just tie two belt loops together with the twine."

"I only have long underwear in my backpack." Banks said as he started unbuttoning his shirt.

Vittles gave a loud laugh and said, "This ain't no fashion show, so wear 'em. In the mean time, I'll rustle up some clean dud's fer the boy here."

As Vittles looked for clothing, David stood by the glowing stove enjoying the warmth. He was hungry but so tired that his eyes ached. A few minutes later the trapper returned and handed him a pair of red long johns, and the young man quickly changed.

As soon as David had changed, Vittles pointed to two bunks built into the sides of his cabin and said, "I used to have a partner, until he tried to play tag with a grizzly bear and lost the game. There are two beds there, so get some sleep."

Three hours later, Banks woke smelling the food cooking on the stove. The ever present coffee pot was perking and Vittles was standing by the stove stirring his stew. David was still sleeping.

"Yer awake now, huh? This stew'll be done in about thirty more minutes, so get a cup off the sink over there and pour ya some coffee. The sourdough bread will be done directly."

"Thanks. Do you have an emergency radio here by chance?"

"Nope, don't like 'em at all. As a matter of fact, I don't like most electronic gadgets, but I do have a reg'lar radio that runs on batteries."

"Do you listen to it often?"

Vittles gave a cackle and replied, "During supper I usually listen to the news, just so I have an idear what all them fools in the lower forty-eight are doin'. Or what people in other parts of the world are doin' to hurt and kill each other. See, John, I came out heah to be left alone and to live a quiet life."

"I can understand that. But, what if there is an emergency or you need help?"

"I've a dog team and if need be I can be at a Native village down the river in about two hours, if the river is frozen. I don't worry much about those kinds of things, not really. I fig'er the good Lord has a plan for me, so what happens is his will."

Banks thought for a moment and then asked, "Can we listen to the news tonight during supper?"

"Why shore, I ain't got no gripes 'bout doin' that. Now, wake that boy and let's eat."

During dinner, they listened to an easy listening station that played what Banks called elevator music. It was mostly piano music or soft and easy instrumentals. While it was relaxing, it was not a station Banks would have picked, he liked hard rock and roll or country and western music.

When the news came on, David and Banks listened as the station reported, "The United States Air Force, Search and Rescue Squadron at Elmendorf Air Force Base, stated today that once the weather clears, rescue flights will continue for the missing son of the late Doctor James Wade. David Wade, the doctor's son, has been missing since the crash of the Wade family's private plane over a week ago. The plane crashed in remote mountains southwest of Anchorage and rescue attempts are hampered by poor weather. Stay tuned to WWX 92 FM for global news."

David gave a loud scream of joy, but Banks was silent. He picked up his coffee, took a small sip and then said, "It may be a while yet before they come. Right now they can't get airborne."

Vittles turned the radio off, gave a crooked grin and said, "Yer both safe heah, so relax, John. When they come you'll be healthy, so all ya have to do is wait."

Banks grinned back at Vittles and said, "In the morning we have some signals to make. I want a large X made out of snow blocks constructed, some fires ready to light, and from now on during the day we have to listen for aircraft in good weather."

Vittles stood, walked to the sink and pulled out a large piece of raw meat. Placing it in a huge pot and covering it with a clean dishcloth, he said, "Tomorrow we'll have bear steaks fer dinner. I got me a brown bear late this season, so it will be better fixin's than stew."

The rest of the evening Banks and David spent looking at magazines Vittles had in a box under his bed. Some of the publications were over forty years old and the trapper said the cabin used to belong to his dad. After his father died, he'd moved here enjoying the solitude.

"How long you been here?" David looked up from a magazine he was looking through.

"Well, near as I can guess almost twenty years. I was thirty when I came out with Franklin, he's the man the bear killed, and I've been alone the last five years."

"How in the world do you survive out here?"

"About six times a year a bush pilot friend of mine drops off some supplies I can't grow, like salt, pepper, flour and whatnot. During the summer, I have me a big garden, and I grow a lot of veggies fer the comin' winter. I can most of 'em in Mason jars and if ya look on the shelf in the kitchen you'll see 'em."

"Don't you ever get bored?" Banks asked as he placed his magazine on the bed covers.

"Yep, I get bored during the middle of winter. I usually take my dog team into Anchorage for the annual fur rendezvous and spend a week there selling pelts and my wood carvings."

"Could we do that now?" David asked in an excited voice.

"No, son, the river ain't froze hard 'nough yet. See, if we tried it now we might crack through the ice and end up dead."

"Any idea how much longer until the ice is thick enough to travel on?" Banks asked, suddenly interested.

"It's hard to say, really. It depends a lot on how cold it gets and how long it stays cold. If yer thinkin' what I think ya are, it'll be at least another month or so. By then you'll be long gone."

"I hope so, but I can't really say until we're talking to the aircraft. Sometimes in search and rescue things happen, so it's best to prepare for all situations."

"I hear ya, but with all the modern contraptions they got these days, I 'spect you'll be gone soon," Vittles said, and then gave a big smile.

"Do you have anything else to do here besides magazines?" David asked.

"Shore, under the other bunk is boxes and boxes of books. I have classics by Edgar Rice Burroughs, O. Henry, James Fenimore Cooper, and a bunch more by other writers. I'll bet there must be fifty books or more under that bed."

"So, you read a lot?" David looked up at the old trapper with questioning eyes.

"Uh-huh and its good fer a feller to read a lot too, especially then the snow starts to fly."

"Vittles, do you mind if I asked you a question about your past?" David asked.

"No, son, ask away."

"What did you do before you became a trapper?"

Vittles laughed, shook his head and said, "Well, in my other life I was a university professor, and I taught literature in Florida. I grew tired of the rat race and came here."

"No!"

"Yep, I surely did. I taught for a little over ten years and then one day I asked myself why. See, I loved teaching, but I was in a rat race along with millions of other folks. Oh, I still love books, its people I don't care much for. So, when a man murdered my wife during a bank robbery, I just gave up on society. I thought if I came up here for a few months, I'd get over my grief. Well, I did get over my hurt, but I lost any urge to move back. I fell in love with the mountains and tundra of Alaska."

"Looks like you found a new lover, old timer," Banks stated and smiled warmly at the trapper.

Vittles laughed, shook his head and said, "Nothing can ever take the place of my Linda, but I understand what ya mean. I've given my heart to the frozen north land and have a love for it that equals the love a man feels for any woman. I can't really explain it, but I guess most Alaskans know what I mean. This is one state ya either love or ya hate."

Banks chuckled and said, "I like it most of the time, but the last few nights were pretty cold out on the open tundra. And, I'm sure David here had a rougher time of it than I did, because he didn't have the right clothing."

"It was cold, but I knew what to do and I did it. I missed hot food the most though, and maybe sleeping warm," David spoke as he stared off into space, remembering the cold nights alone.

"It's time for us to get some sleep. It's going to be a long day tomorrow, because we have a lot of work to do." Banks said as he stretched out on the bunk. Then thinking, he asked, "Vittles, where will you sleep?"

"Heck, I'll make me a pallet right by the stove and sleep as warm as toast."

"Night, Vittles, and thanks for the help." David said from his bunk.

"Good night, David, and ya get some rest."

CHAPTER 13

Captains Zlotkowski and Baldwin were in the air moving toward the crash site. While the snow continued to fall, it was very light. The winds had stopped, but the sky had not completely cleared. The sun was peeking through in a few scattered spots. As they neared the site of Doctor Wade's crashed plane, pararescueman William Price went over his gear. While the young Technical Sergeant did not expect to be on the ground, if he was needed he'd not be able to check his equipment before he left the aircraft. Satisfied his gear was in place and in good condition; he leaned back in the orange troop seat and listened to the aircraft communications.

"Zee, let's do a couple of circles over the site to give Banks time to come up voice on the radio."

"Not a problem, we can do that. Pilot to crew, watch outside the aircraft for any signals Banks may have out. There is always a chance his PRC-90 is broken or has a dead battery."

A few minutes later, Baldwin spoke once more, "Should be getting his radio on guard by now, but nothing."

"Price, you get ready to go down if we don't see any signals or hear his radio. Our estimated time of arrival over the crash site is two mikes."

Price knew two mikes meant two minutes, so he made sure his gear was secure and replied, "Roger, understand and I'm ready."

"First, we'll circle a few times." Zee said as he placed the chopper in a slow lazy circle over the crash site.

After a few minutes, Zee called, "Rescue Center, Save One, requesting to lower a P.J. to the ground. Currently we have no contact with Angel One or the survivor."

"Save One, Rescue Center, any signs of signals or weak radio transmissions?"

"Negative, Center, nothing at all."

Colonel Wilcox thought seriously about the dangers of putting another man on the ground and was concerned about the weather. The last thing he wanted to do was to place a second P.J. in danger if the aircraft had to return to the base quickly. *Banks must be dead or hurt, or else why doesn't he have a signal out? And, according to the life support section, he should still have some radio battery life left in his first battery,* the colonel thought as he shook his head.

"Roger, understand no signs of the survivor or Angel One."

The wind started to pick up and the chopper wobbled as Zee fought the controls to keep the aircraft stable. Snow started falling harder and it was becoming harder to see out of the windscreen.

Wilcox battled the decision, but finally said, "Save One, Rescue Center, negative, I repeat, negative on lowering another P.J.. Rescue 26 will not be lowered under any circumstance, unless you hear a radio or see signals. Please acknowledge, over."

"Zee, ya have to let me try to find John and that kid!" Price, Rescue 26, suddenly spoke on the aircraft intercom.

"You heard the boss, Price, no way."

"Come on, Zee, they'll die if they stay out here much longer."

"I don't make the rules, but I have to follow them Price and the answer is still no."

"Save One, did you copy our last transmission?"

"Roger, Rescue 26 will remain in the aircraft. Center, the weather is turning rough out here with high winds and more snow. What's the forecast?"

"Wait one."

Zee knew the Colonel would contact the weather section and then pass the word.

"Roger."

A few minutes later Rescue Center was back, "Save One, Center, return to base. The weather is changing so fast you may have a hard time the last few miles. Another front just moved in and it will get rougher before it gets better."

"Understand, Rescue Center. We are to abort this mission and return to base."

"Roger that Save One, you tried, but let's call it a day."

"Save One, returning to base."

As the aircraft broke from its low circle over the crash site, no one noticed the large snow signal near the trees a few miles from the wreckage. All eyes were on the ground below the chopper and no one expected Banks or David to have moved. It was a sad crew aboard the helicopter as it leveled off in flight and started back to Elmendorf. Rotor blast, from the helicopter, blew the note Banks had left in his shelter high into the air. The note had his compass heading and explained why he was leaving the crash scene.

After debriefing Zlotkowski and the crew, Colonel Wilcox met with General Moores to discuss the aborted mission. After saluting the senior officer and being instructed to have a seat, Wilcox explained what had happened. The General didn't say a word as the Colonel spoke, but he was thinking hard on the choices he had to make.

"Do you have any questions, sir?" Wilcox asked as he met the General's eyes.

"Frank, I don't know how much longer I can keep Headquarters Air Force off of our backs. Headquarters Search and Rescue at Scott Air Force Base are behind us, but even they're getting to the point that something will be said in a day or two. We've spent a lot of money on our rescue attempts and I'm not sure how much longer we'll be able to keep it up. But, why do you think Sergeant Banks didn't signal your chopper?"

"One of three things happened sir and I'm sure of it. Banks might be dead, he could be severely injured, or he might have moved."

"Of course these are only guesses, right?"

"Yes sir, I have nothing concrete to base my statement on except years of rescue experience."

General Moores smiled and replied, "Frank, I think your P.J. and the Wade boy have moved. I know Banks has been trained to stay at a crash site, but with the bad weather we've had recently, he may have been forced to move. Plus, I was talking to a friend of mine over the weekend and he told me the area of the crash has a few old trappers in it. They may have met a trapper or moved to a trapper's cabin, maybe. Then again, there are natives in the area too."

"So, what do we do now, sir?"

"I see us as having three choices in the matter. We can send in rescue teams by dog team or snowmobile and can move them near the crash site by C-130 cargo planes. We can wait for the weather to break and then go back out by choppers, only this time we'll lower rescue teams. Or, we can simply forget about the rescue and get on with our lives."

Colonel Wilcox quickly said, "Sir, I don't think leaving one of our own behind would be a good decision. I mean, what would that be telling the other P.J.'s who may have to be left behind in the future? No, sir, leaving Banks would be a grave mistake in my eyes."

The General gave a flat chuckle and replied, "Relax Frank, I only said those were our options. I have no intentions of leaving the P.J. or the survivor behind, because I'm a firm believer in finishing what I start. You wait for the weather to clear, have five qualified members form a rescue team, and be ready to go. As soon as the weather section can give you three or four days of good weather I want that team at the crash site. If you feel the need, form two teams of men."

"I understand, sir, and I'll have them ready to go."

"Well," the General said with a grin, "why are you still in that chair? Get out and get your folks ready to go, Colonel, and if you need anything or anyone gives you a hard time, just let me know."

As Frank Wilcox stood, saluted and left the room, General Moores thought as he leaned back in his chair and closed his eyes, *Frank, I hope this weather clears soon, or I may be force by Headquarters to terminate this mission. I don't want to do that, I really don't.*

* * *

Banks had seen the rescue chopper just as it banked to return to base. He ran to his signal fires, dropped a match in the first pile of brush, picked up a burning brand and set the other two piles of pine branches on fire. A dense orange color reached for the sky as the Sergeant ignited a smoke flare and held it so it would rise with the smoke from his fire. Removing his survival radio, he said, "Save One, Angel One, do you copy, over?"

No response, "Save One, this is Angel One, do you copy?"

Still no answer, so Banks moved the transmit button to "beeper" and let the radio send out a steady beeping noise on the emergency guard frequency. The aircraft should have heard Banks transmitting with the radio and been able to fix his position after a few seconds, but the aircraft never changed course.

Banks, feeling disappointed over not being able to contact the aircraft, knew they'd be back. One thing he'd learned in the Air Force, they never left a person behind until they'd done all they could to get them out. Looking up at the rolling gray clouds, he suspected the chopper was returning to base due to weather. He let his fires burn down, covered the glowing embers with snow, and made three new ones for the next time an aircraft neared.

"How come they didn't hear you on the radio?" David asked from beside Banks.

"Weather can affect the radio transmission, just like a weak battery can. I'm not sure why they couldn't hear me, but I'll keep the spare battery on me next time, so I can change the battery if I don't get a response. Surely one of them will work."

"I wasn't sure if they'd see the smoke, since they were probably looking at the crash site, so I hoped the radio was our way home. Dog gone it!"

Banks put his left hand on David's shoulder and said, "Chill man, they'll be back. Right now, we have a warm place to sleep, hot food, shelter, and all the comforts of home. Heck, we could live for years out here if we had to do it."

"Years! Without a television, games, or my computer? I don't mind reading for a few days, but I miss calling my friends to talk, going to the mall, or just chatting online."

Banks laughed, shook his head and said, "David, those are fun things to do, except right now we're concerned about our survival. The search aircraft will be back and when it does we'll be ready."

Vittles came walking up with a fresh fox skin in his right hand. Turning to Banks he asked, "Was that a chopper I heard a few minutes ago?"

"Uh-huh, but they didn't spot my signals or talk with me."

"How come? Ya got a radio."

"Not sure why Vittles, but they didn't hear the radio or see my smoke or flare."

"Atmospheric conditions most likely." The old trapper said.

"Yep, that's what I figured too." Banks replied as he zipped up the small pocket on his SRU-21/P survival vest that held his radio.

David looked at the trapper with a confused look and asked, "Atmospheric conditions? I don't understand."

Vittles chuckled and said, "Our atmosphere has all sorts of electrical currents moving around in it. Now, Alaska has more than most. That's what gives us the northern lights, and it makes it tough to transmit with a radio or to receive."

"I understand, but the chopper was close."

Vittles pushed his hat back on his head and said, "Could be the batteries in the radio are too weak or maybe there was a noise in the cockpit of the chopper that drowned out the radio. I ain't got any way of knowin', but they'll be back."

"John says that too, but how do you really know?"

137

"Way back in 1968, I was in the Republic of Vietnam with the Marines for fourteen months, and we never left a man behind that was yet alive. And, I can only remember two times we left dead men and that was because the enemy wouldn't let us get close enough to recover the bodies."

"I heard once the Marines have never left a man or body behind." David said as he tried to remember where he'd heard the comment.

Vittles laughed and said, "That's an unofficial Marine Corp motto. They've had to leave a few behind, but not often. See, in the service we tried to take care of each other, and some of us were closer than brothers could ever be. So, when one of us was injured or killed we tried our best to get 'em out, even at the risk of our own lives."

"I hate to break this up, but we need to get back to the cabin. I'm freezing to death standing out here while Vittles tells us war stories," Banks said, and then laughed as he moved toward the log structure.

Entering the cabin, they immediately felt the warmth the small sheet metal woodstove was producing. As usual, it was glowing red on one side and it seemed to David the stove burned wood almost as fast as he could stack it in the corner. When he'd been out in the bush surviving, he would have welcomed the heat, but now that he was safe he felt Vittles allowed the small cabin to get too hot at times.

Hours later, after a dinner of bear steaks, boiled potatoes, and cornbread, the three of them read books by lantern light. David had never been around lanterns or the old time lamps that burned kerosene, but Vittles had them both. Of the two, the young man favored the kerosene lamps because he thought they were neat and gave off more light. First Vittles drifted off to sleep and then John followed him, as David continued to read. It was hours later when the young man decided it was time for bed and as he stood to place his book on a table, David felt his book hit something and then heard breaking glass.

Quickly looking down at the noise, he saw the lamp had fallen to the floor of the cabin and flames were now moving up the blanket on his bed. Pulling his pillow, David attempted to fight the fire, but to no avail. Filled with panic, he screamed for help. The wood of the cabin was seasoned and as dry as the desert sands. By the time Banks awoke and moved toward the bed the whole wall was engulfed in flames.

Thick gray-black smoke filled the small structure and Vittles called out, "Get out. Grab blankets, your gear, and all the clothing you can find! Hurry, this place will go up like a match box!"

Grabbing his coat, boots, two blankets and a butcher knife from the table, David ran out into the frigid arctic air. The sky was clear, with stars sparkling overhead, but no one noticed. Banks picked up his clothing, survival gear, and his boots, but he could not stand the smoke long enough to get anything else.

Moving out into the clearing in front of the cabin, they watched as flames consumed all that Vittles owned. Long red-orange fingers of fire reached for the sky and dense black smoke boiled over the burning cabin. The flames had spread so quickly that David was amazed by the speed and intensity of the fire.

"Ya knocked a lamp over, didn't you son?" The old trapper asked David.

Looking over at the old man, David could see light from the fire on his face as he replied, "Yes, it's my fault."

Vittles grinned and said, "Nope, the fault was mine. I should have made you go to bed when I did, but I didn't do that. Kerosene lamps are dangerous and in the old days, many a home burned down just like this one is. And, you said you'd never been around the lamps before, so I should have known better."

Banks interrupted, "Look, it doesn't matter whose fault it is, we need to find shelter and do it now. It's near ten below out here, so every minute counts."

"Put yer coat on, David, and ya two foller me. I got a small building out back that I keep my furs in until I can get 'em to market. It's small, no stove, but it has a lamp and we can make a stove from a coffee can or two I have there," Vittles said and then started moving around to the back of his flaming cabin.

The building was small, maybe ten feet by ten feet, but it had a roof and was better than anything they could make. David was shivering by the time they reached the crudely made structure, and knew he'd warm up once they got a fire going. He watched as Vittles took an old coffee can, turned it upside down, and made a small fire in the can. He winked at David and said, "Now, this ain't the safest way to make a fire, but we'll be safe from carbon monoxide poisoning because this place has a thousand small cracks that let the wind in. The key to a fire in a closed shelter is to keep it well ventilated."

"I know. I got a bad headache on the way here because I forgot to make a vent hole in my snow shelter," David replied remembering that night.

"Lots of things in the bush can kill a person, from the weather to the critters. The key is to try to learn all ya can before you leave a town. Each year people come up here expecting one thing, but finding another. Our mountains are beautiful, but they'll kill an unprepared or ignorant person in no time."

"How's our food supply?" Banks asked as he moved some animal pelts and sat on a wooden bench.

"Got lots of meat in the cache, but that's 'bout it. The fire burned up most of the veggies and canned goods. I'm just glad I was able to grab my two guns before I ran from the cabin. I keep some ammunition out here and some in my cache, so I always have some when I need it. I'm semi-prepared for a fire."

"In what ways?" Banks asked.

"I've got extra clothing, knives, one gun, matches, fuel and some other things in the cache, but not a lot. Just enough to keep a man alive fer a short spell, but that don't include no vegetables at all."

"Ok, so we'll have to find something to fight off scurvy. We can drink pine needle tea, but it's a bit on the sour side. Nonetheless, it will give us the needed vitamin C." Banks gave a grimace as he thought of drinking the tea.

"Yep, we can do that and that's smart thinkin' if we're here fer a spell."

"Well," Banks said as he gave a false smile, "things could be a lot worse."

"Let's just hope things stay as they are, because this is rough enough for me. Looks like I'll have to fly back to Anchorage with you and spend the winter. I lost all the food, supplies, and pretty much all I own a few minutes ago." Vittles stated as he lit the tinder with cold fingers and watch the flames grow in his makeshift stove.

CHAPTER 14

In General Moores' office the curtains were open, allowing the sun to shine in as two men sat talking. Coffee was in the hands of both and the atmosphere was as relaxing as it ever gets in a General's office.

"Frank, get your rescue teams moving as fast as you can. The weather forecasters assured me of five or six days of good weather to get to the Wade crash site and find those two."

Colonel Wilcox grinned and replied, "I've already alerted my crews, and they're on standby to lift off as we speak."

The General's face grew grim as he said, "Frank, this will be our last attempt. If the teams should fail to find Banks and David, well, we'll not get another chance. I've been notified by phone from Major General Thomas that this will be it. He thinks, and I agree with him, that the weather is too severe and the cost too high to keep searching. You've got five or six days— find them."

Standing, Frank said as he saluted, "I'll find them, sir."

Once outside the General's door, Colonel Wilcox began running to his office. Standing by his desk, he picked up the phone, dialed a number and said, "Zee, it's a go. Get the two choppers ready along with the rescue teams. As soon as you're ready, give me a call at the command post to make sure it's still on. At that point I'll give you a go ahead or abort."

"Yes, sir! I'd imagine we'll be ready to lift off within twenty minutes. The teams have the gear loaded and all of them are in the alert building."

On his way to the command post, Colonel Wilcox noticed it was still very cold, but the sun was shining and there was not a cloud in the sky. *Please, God, let this rescue work,* he thought as he entered the building.

The command post, filled with men and women coordinating maintenance for all the aircraft assigned to the base, was busy. People came and went, always in a rush. The aircraft could radio the command post and talk about aircraft problems or discuss missions if need be. Colonel Wilcox sat in his seat, asked for a cup of coffee, and waited.

On the flight line, the two choppers were loaded and ready to go before the captain transmitted, "Rescue Center, this is Save One. We're ready for liftoff."

"Roger, Save One, this is Rescue Center, the mission is a go."

"I read you five by five and understand the mission is a go."

"Affirmative Save One, good luck and good hunting!"

"Will do. This is Save One, I'm switching to the tower now Rescue Center. Thanks for the luck!"

The Colonel leaned back in his chair, enjoyed his coffee and thought, *nothing to do now, but wait.*

* * *

Zee could feel the excitement as the rescue team members prepared to exit the aircraft at the crash site. The members gave thumbs up and replied, "Okay!" as

Zee called them by name asking if they were ready to go. This is why I fly in rescue, the pilot thought as he hovered over the crashed Wade aircraft. Ropes were thrown out of the door, on both sides of the chopper, d-rings were snapped shut around the ropes and the men started repelling down to the ground.

Once the last man was safely on the ground, Zee heard, "Save One this is Rescue 26, the team is on the ground and you're clear to liftoff."

"Roger Rescue 26, understand I am cleared to liftoff. Center, this is Save One, the team is on the ground. I'll say again, Rescue 26 and the team are on the ground."

"Save One, good news. You are to move off slightly and circle until Rescue 26 contacts you. What's your fuel status?"

"Long time left on gas, Save Center, I'll let you know when I'm getting low. Save Two, has also just landed their team. Both teams are on the ground."

"Copy, Safe One, understand both teams on the ground."

On the ground Technical Sergeant Price, Rescue 26 team leader, listened as the two choppers flew away. He knew they'd be circling nearby and if he needed them all he had to do was radio one of them. Looking around the crash site, there were no tracks in the snow. From all appearances, the place was as clean as a whistle.

"Richard, take two men and check out the top of this mountain. Once on top, scan the area below 360 degrees and look for smoke or signs of life." Staff Sergeant Richard Usher was the team leader for the second search group, Save 27.

"Not a problem, Bill, we'll radio you if we see anything. Lopez, you take point and Bagley, you're my slack man. Let's move, people."

"Save One, this is Rescue 26, how about one of you flying around down low out there and looking for signs of life?" Price radioed Zee, hoping they'd spot some smoke or see a signal of some sort.

"Rog, we'll both do it. If you need us, remember our motto."

Price laughed and said, "I remember, 'I call and you haul!'"

A laugh sounded over the radio and then Zee replied, "We're going low level now."

The birds were quickly spotted by Price as they dropped down low to fly over the tundra, searching in a very well organized pattern. They were flying box like patterns, to cover as much of the terrain as possible. However, they were well west of where David Wade sat shivering in the cold cabin.

"Rescue 26, this is Rescue 27, nothing moving on the tundra."

"Copy Rescue 27, return to the crash site."

Where could they have gone? Are they still on the mountain? Or, did they move out onto the open tundra. I noticed a few groups of trees a few miles from here, so they might be there. But, smoke should have been seen by Richard, Sergeant Price thought as he pulled his ski cap down tighter on his head to block the cold light wind.

Once Usher returned, he and Price looked the map of the area over closely. Marked off in one thousand meter areas, the topographical map showed the mountain, and a complete range of mountains to the north. To the west and east was open tundra with small groups of trees at odd intervals. It was rough country and both of the rescue men knew it was unlikely that Banks or the Wade boy still lived. Since it was not uncommon for the nights in the area to be twenty degrees below zero or more, the average person would freeze to death in a day, two at the most.

"Save One, Rescue 26, do you have a visual on anything?"

"Rescue 26, negative." He heard Zee's voice come back with a response quickly.

"Save One, I'd like to move Rescue 27 off to the east to check the tundra while I move off to the west and check the trees."

"Roger, copy." Zee answered and then came back a second later with, "Save Two we will do 360's off to the east and I'll do the same on the west side."

Sergeant Price knew the aircraft would fly circles over them, so in case they found the survivors or needed help they'd be close enough to communicate by radio or land quickly. "Copy, Save One, we're moving now."

Turning to his rescue team, Sergeant Usher said, "Saddle up, we're moving out onto the tundra to the east."

No complaint was heard as the men adjusted their gear, lowered their facemasks, and began the hump down the mountain. It was just a few minutes later when Sergeant Price and his men started down the west side. The going was slow, due to newly fallen snow, and more than once a man fell on the slippery surface. Not long after making the bottom of the mountain, the Radio Telephone Operator (RTO) moved up beside Price and handed him the headset as he said, "It's Save One."

"Save One, this is Rescue 26, over."

"Rescue 26, we are bingo on fuel and need to return to base.

"Copy, you are returning to base."

"Roger that, and don't expect us back until daylight."

147

"You have a nice trip back Save One, and I'll catch you in the morning."

"On the behalf of my crew, Safe One, we'd like to thank you for flying with us on this fine day. We hope you'll remember us for your future flying needs. Good luck Rescue 26, out."

Price chuckled and thought the humor was a symbol of the type of men he was working with. Even under severe stress, they kept their humor, while performing a serious and potentially deadly mission. Great men, he thought as he readjusted his web belt as he walked and listened to the sound of the choppers growing fainter.

By dusk, the men reached the open tundra and began to set up camp. Unlike David and Sergeant Banks, they brought lightweight tents and other special gear for the mission, so they did not make a snow shelter. The rescue teams gear was light and designed for arctic explorers and rescue teams.

Over a heated MRE, Price glanced over at Airman Tony Baird and noticed the fatigue on the young man's face. Finally, Price asked, "You hangin' in there, Tony?"

"I'm doing fine. I just find walking in all of this deep snow to be more difficult than I thought it would be."

Price laughed and then replied, "It's hard on a man and more than one person has died from a heart attack walking in this stuff. By the way, I know this is your first mission, so it seems harder than it really is."

"I'm in good physical shape; just new to the job is all! For some reason, training didn't seem this rough." Tony said with a laugh.

Price gave a light grin and replied, "Tony, your training was much more difficult than this, physically. The mental aspects of this mission make it rougher.

We all want to find Wade and Banks, so the emotional stress is what you're dealing with right now. And, the mental part of the mission can make you as tired as the physical efforts can."

Tony met the eyes of the older rescue man and said, "Uh-huh, I think you're right. I know Sergeant Banks real well, and I'd like to be part of the group that finds him."

"Maybe it'll be us or maybe it'll be Ushers' team, but Tony, keep in mind we may never find a sign of either one of these guys. This country is hard on people and its valley's and canyons are filled with unburied bones of those who made a single simple mistake at the wrong time."

Looking down at his boots, Tony didn't look up, even though he could feel the eyes of Sergeant Price on him. Finally, he said softly, "Sergeant Price, there's always a chance we won't find these two, but it won't be because we didn't try."

Price reached over, patted the younger man on the shoulder, and replied, "We never leave a man behind that we can recover and you know that. So, you just keep our motto in mind as you walk tomorrow, 'That Others May Live.' We're out here, hopefully, to save two lives and that makes our mission special. At least nobody is shooting at us."

Tony gave a slight grin, looked up and said, "I'll do that Sergeant."

The next morning, instead of moving toward the tree line where David and the rest were sheltered, Sergeant Price led his men to the southwest and another tree line that was about two miles closer. He fully intended to move toward David's trees, but he'd start that search the next day. Price knew most survivors moved in circles or made their way to the closest shelter, so the tree line he'd picked that morning made sense to him professionally. As he walked, Price prayed that David had met with Sergeant Banks, because that would greatly increase his chances of survival. Even without any survival gear, Banks was fully capable of surviving in the arctic and had done it often enough in training.

As they walked, Price called out, "Remember to keep a watch on your water intake and check for dehydration at each break."

All of the members of the rescue team knew dark urine was a sure sign of dehydration and that in cold weather most people had a tendency to drink less water than normal. Often, when they took breaks, the men would drink hot water to make sure their bodies were getting enough fluids. Besides, the hot water helped to keep their body heat up.

It was less than an hour after dawn when the RTO moved up beside Price, during a short break, handed him the headset and grinned as he said, "Guess who?"

"Save One, Rescue 26, how do you read me?" Sergeant Price spoke into the small microphone.

"Five by five, Rescue 26, and I hope your night was restful."

"Not bad. I complained to the manager about the lack of heat, but he didn't seem interested."

Zee, who fought hard to hold back his laughter said, "Rescue 26, we'll 360 over both teams as long as we can. Colonel Wilcox has two other birds scheduled to take over when we bingo on fuel."

"Copy Save One, out." Price spoke, handed the headset to his RTO and then turning to his team he said, "Saddle up and let's move. I want to be in that tree line before noon."

The team reached the trees well before noon, but there was no sign of anyone having been in the area. It was hours later, over a hot cup of coffee, and as the sun went down that Price said, "Any of you guys have any ideas?"

"They might be in the next group of trees to the northwest." Airman First Class Chip Brown spoke as he raised his steaming coffee cup.

"They could be." Price admitted.

"Look," Sergeant Bill Lavet, the assistant team leader said, "we have to face the fact they might well both be dead too. Now, don't everyone jump on me, but it's more than likely they haven't survived the cold."

Price gave a shallow smile and replied, "Well, it makes no difference if they've survived or not as far as I'm concerned. I intend to keep looking until I find them, their bodies, or I'm called back by Rescue Center." He noticed Tony Baird give a big smile.

Lavet look around the small group. "I'm not saying we quit, and I'm not a quitter. I just meant we are looking for survivors, when maybe we should be looking for bodies. No one has seen any signs of life and as much as I like John Banks, well, there is a better than average chance he didn't make it. Besides, what are the odds a young boy like David Wade surviving the period he was alone before John was even put on the ground."

The team grew quiet and after a short time Price said, as he looked over at Lavet, "Bill, I hope you're wrong, but you could be right. The problem, if they have died, is finding the remains in all this fresh snow."

"There aren't any remains where we've been so far." Airman Samuel Jenkins, the dog handler, said as he placed his empty cup in his rucksack. "If there had been, Max would have moved toward them."

Max was the big German Sheppard trained in rescue and recovery. Part of the dog's job was to find survivors, but another part was locating remains of those who did not survive. He'd been with them from the beginning, so maybe there was still hope for David Wade and John Banks.

"Good point, Sam, and from now on I want you and Max on point, though we'll take turns breaking the snow on the trail so you don't wear yourself out." Price said with a grin as he thought, *Max, you could actually end up being a real lifesaver in this situation.*

The next morning, just as a false dawn broke off to the east, Zee was back on the radio, "Rescue 26, this is Save One."

"Copy, Save One, go ahead." Price spoke as he unzipped his coat a few inches to allow his body heat and moisture to escape.

"I've got some bad news, Rescue 26, the mission is called off. There is another bad front moving in, and Headquarters Air Force has ordered the teams to return to base. I repeat you are to return to base."

Price didn't answer immediately because he felt a mixture of anger and shock. They all knew if they returned now they'd never come back. For a moment he considered not responding, knowing he could always say later he'd not received the last message from Zlotkowski and blame it on radio problems. But, like the professional he was, he replied, "Copy, Save One, has Rescue 27 been informed?"

"Roger that and they didn't take it well."

"Understand that Save One. Give me five Mikes to prepare a LZ."

"Roger, five mikes, and I have you visual Rescue 26. Our ETA is less than five Mikes"

Five minutes later a bright orange panel was on the snow and the men lined up to load onto the chopper. Airman Baird pulled a MK-13 Mod-O flare from his survival vest and held it at the ready in his right hand. The smoke from the flare, once popped, would indicate wind direction to the chopper pilot and make his landing safer.

"Save One, Rescue 26, popping smoke now." Price spoke as he nodded to Baird and pointed with his right index finger. The young airman pulled the metal o-ring and there came a slight *fizzing* sound as the flare ignited. Bright orange smoke shot out from the end of the flare and was very noticeable against the white background.

"Roger, we see your smoke and have you in sight."

No one spoke on the way home and it bothered Sergeant Price that they'd not been able to search the tree line furthest away from the mountain. While he'd seen no smoke or other indications anyone was there, something about those trees now bothered him. *I hope to God they were not in those trees,* he thought as he looked out of the chopper window at the frozen ground below.

The air was rough and the chopper bounced as Zee sat in the front left seat and felt frustrated because the mission aborted. As a rescue pilot, he was willing to risk his life and the life of his crews, if there was a remote chance to save a person, but he couldn't disobey an order. Before he was a rescue pilot, he was an officer in the United States Air Force and as such, he had no choice but to return to base. He'd flown countless missions and most had resulted in survivors being rescued, while others hadn't ended so nicely. But, in all of his years flying in Rescue and Recovery, this was the first time no signs of possible survivors had been found. It was as if the mountain had simply swallowed Banks and Wade alive, leaving no sign of them ever being there.

CHAPTER 15

Snow was falling as Colonel Wilcox walked from the Command Post to his office. His mind was not on the weather or at least it wasn't any longer; other than being very cold, the weather no longer had any impact. Once the mission to find Banks and David had been recalled, the weather no longer mattered to him; instead, the reality of leaving a comrade behind had come to the front of his mind. Never in his many years of service, except for once in combat, had he ever failed to find a survivor or their remains. He felt a mixture of anger and frustration, and then realized the rescue teams, pilots, and everyone involved in the rescue attempt must feel the same way. But, none of them had had a choice, because the Air Force had stopped the mission based on the safety of the pilots and rescue teams. He understood the safety matter and then thought, *Perhaps I'm too personally involved in all of this. If Jim hadn't been a friend or if I had not known David, would I still feel this way? How can I tell this to Cathy? How can I tell her I can no longer search for her missing son?*

Once in his office, the Colonel called home and informed his wife that the mission was finished and no sign found of either person.

"Frank, can't y'all go back out once the weather breaks?" Carol asked.

"No, honey, the mission is scrubbed for good. The experts seem to think there is no chance either of them are still alive. I called the arctic survival experts at Fairchild Air Force Base and while they didn't come right out and say it, I got the feeling they agreed. They kept talking about body heat, hypothermia, calorie and protein intake, frostbite and a whole bunch of other stuff. According to them, if both Banks and David were very lucky they might still be alive, but it was unlikely."

"Frank, how can we break this to Cathy?"

"I don't have any idea. The woman has already lost her husband, and now I have to tell her I've left her only son in the mountains."

"She'll go to pieces, Frank, so you'd better show up with her minister and a doctor."

"I'll stop by on the way home and get Pastor Lucas. In the mean time, you contact her therapist and have him meet me here at my office. I'll notify the front gate he's coming so he'll have no problems getting an entry pass."

"Frank?"

"Yep?"

"How are you takin' all of this?"

"Hard Carol, but I'll survive. I still think those two are alive and I have absolutely no facts to base my feelings on. There were no signs of either of them, but I have no choice now; I have to stop the search. Oh, Carol?"

"Yes?"

"I'll be home as soon as I can, but way before the six o'clock news. The FAA, Civil Air Patrol, and the Air Force have scheduled a press release for that time. It'll be short and sweet, but it'd hard on Cathy, so let's keep her from the television if we can."

"Frank, I love you."

"I love you too, baby, but I have to get back to work," Colonel Wilcox spoke and then hung up the phone. He closed his eyes, tilted his head back, and felt mentally exhausted.

"Sir," Sergeant Donaldson spoke as he entered the office, "I've got you a cup of coffee and I wanted to remind you of the mission debrief with General Moores in ten minutes."

Opening his eyes and leaning forward, Colonel Wilcox said, "Thanks Jim, for both the coffee and the reminder. How long have you been in rescue?"

"Twenty-one years, sir."

"Ever leave anyone behind?"

"We had to do it once in Vietnam and it was hard to do. I was the P.J. on that mission, and I was looking out the door and right into that man's eyes when the pilot told him we had to leave. I'll never forget the look on his face, never."

"Why did you abort the mission?"

"We'd already lost two choppers attempting to get him out and even as we hovered over him and I prepared to go down to get him, we started taking ground fire. It was pretty heavy, and I could hear the bullets striking the aircraft. I guess the AC had to make a choice and now I think he made the right one, but I didn't at the time. If we had not called off the rescue, all of us, including the survivor might have been killed."

"Was the man later released as a prisoner of war?"

Sergeant Donaldson's eyes grew sad as he slowly shook his head and replied, "No, sir, he was not released at the war's end. He's listed as MIA to this day."

"Thanks again for the coffee, Jim."

"No problem sir, but don't forget your meeting with the boss." Donaldson replied and then left the office.

Entering the General's office a short time later, Wilcox saluted as he approached his commander's desk.

"Frank," General Moores said, "take a seat and be at ease."

"Yes sir," Wilcox replied as he sat in the plush leather chair.

The General didn't speak for a few moments, as if he needed time to organize his thoughts, but finally he said, "You understand why the search has been called off, right?"

"Yes sir, I do."

"Frank, honestly, I don't see any way those two could still be alive. The temperature has been well below zero for weeks, the snow has piled up by the yard, and, well, I think they're dead."

Wilcox moved uncomfortably on his chair as he replied, "Sir, with all respect, I disagree with both you and HQ on this. I think they are still alive, but I will follow orders. I know the search is expensive and we've had no luck, only I don't like the idea of leaving one of our own behind."

General Moores let out a loud sigh, slowly shook his head and said, "Frank, I suspect you're too close to the people you're looking for, but I've told you that before. And, second, I feel you are not looking at this in its proper light. The weather has killed those two by now, regardless of how much you don't want to admit it."

Wilcox did not reply, but he felt anger building inside, *Keep it under control here, because the General is just following orders too,* he thought.

Silence filled the large room, until General Moores said, "I don't want you to leave this meeting with me with a negative attitude, Frank." As he spoke, the General reached into his top drawer, pulled out some papers and said with a smile, "Your promotion to

Brigadier General has just come through, and you're being reassigned to the Air Force Rescue Center at Scott Air Force Base. The promotion is to take effect on the first of May, next year, but you'll be moving in sixty days."

Wilcox was dumbfound, because he'd never expected to ever rise above Major and now he was being notified he had been selected to become a General Officer. As he sat in the chair, unspeaking, the General reached into his drawer once more, pulled out two shiny single stars and tossed them to the Colonel. As he caught them, the General said, "Frank, you deserve this promotion more than any man I know. In all of my years of working with search and rescue, you're the best. Now, let me be the first person to congratulate you on your promotion."

As the General stood, so did Wilcox and they shook hands. Frank finally managed to say in a weak voice, "Thank you, sir."

General Moores gave a light chuckle and said, "Frank, this is the first time I've ever seen you almost speechless. Now, get out of here and back to work. I'll make an announcement about your promotion at the staff meeting on Friday morning."

* * *

Cathy Wade sat crying in her living room as Colonel Wilcox, Carol and Pastor Lucas attempted to comfort her. It had been difficult for Colonel Wilcox to tell her the search had ended, but it had to be done. *Now, she's lost both of the men in her life,* he thought as he met his wife's eyes and slowly shook his head. He nodded toward the kitchen and a few minutes later he was alone with his wife.

He said, "Carol, you stay here with Cathy tonight and I'll see you tomorrow after work. I suspect right now, she'd need all the support she can get."

"Frank, I'll stay with her as long as she needs me, but I think the Air Force has made a mistake in this."

"Mistake or not, Carol, the search has been called off. You have to understand that the Air Force will do anything humanly possible to rescue folks, but once a reasonable period has elapsed or when there is no longer any hope of finding survivors, well, they have no choice but to call the mission off. The cost of this mission alone is into many hundreds of thousands of dollars, and we're no closer to finding David now than when we first started. At some point, a General Officer will usually say, that's enough."

"Speakin' of Generals, tomorrow night let's go by the Officers Club, have dinner and celebrate your promotion. I'm so proud of you, Frank, and I should be with you tonight to share this with you, but I can't."

Colonel Wilcox gave a low chuckle and replied, "Carol, we have a lifetime to share and if you hadn't decided to stay with Cathy, you'd not be the wonderful woman I married. I not only expected you to stay with her, but I want you to stay. She needs you as a friend."

A little later, Colonel Wilcox was sitting at his kitchen table sipping on a cup of coffee as he opened a large box. He only opened this box every few years, when he wanted to remember his military career and the people he had known. The box was filled with photos, medals, and other odds and ends he'd collected over years of service. To most people, it would appear to be a collection of junk and perhaps it was, but it was his junk. All of it had meaning and value to him.

The first photo he pulled out was of him sitting in a rescue chopper in Vietnam. He had been so young then, just a little over twenty, and the eyes of a tired and experienced rescue pilot looked back at him. He remembered well the reason for his fatigue. . .

"Save, this is bamboo echo three, over."

"Go three."

"I got movement to the west, maybe a two hundred meters."

"Roger, copy. Put your head down three, I'll have the fast movers work the area over for you."

"Tango niner four, this is Save. Three has reported movement in the tree line two hundred meters west of his position. What ya got to help him out?"

"Save, Tango niner four, I have some Mark 84's and a little shake and bake."

Wilcox knew the Mark 84 was a five hundred pound bomb and shake and bake was napalm. "Rog, understand, drop the shake and bake in the tree line."

"Copy Save, one shake and bake comin' right up. Tell three to lower his butt, it might get hot down there."

A few seconds later, as the jets turned to approach the target all enemy ground fire stopped. Wilcox quickly moved over the survivor, lowered the rescue collar, and watched as the whole tree line lit up in flames. Within four minutes, the downed pilot was onboard and he pulled to the west, gaining altitude all the while. When they got back to base, the crew chief counted over forty bullet holes in the chopper, and a gunner had a wounded leg he'd not said anything about. The photo brought all of his memories back with vivid clarity.

The remainder of the evening Colonel Wilcox relived most of his career in his mind by looking at old photographs. Some had torn edges and many were black and white, but each held a small part of his memory and past. It was late before he turned off the light and went to bed, wondering how he'd survived long enough to make Captain, much less General.

* * *

The next morning, Wilcox left for work early and as he drove by Cathy's house he said, "God, give her strength, she's a good woman."

The morning was cold, with snow falling gently and a light wind. The temperature was warmer than usual at minus ten. He'd just stepped out of his car when a Captain he knew from the Command Post walked to his side, saluted and then asked, "Did you hear about the beacon reported last night, sir? Seems a—" He never got to finished, because Colonel Wilcox was running as fast as the slippery walkway would allow toward his office.

Entering quickly he asked, "What's this I heard of a beacon being reported last night?"

"We didn't get the word until General Moores called just a few minutes ago. Seems a private pilot was returning from a village when he picked up a weak beacon on guard near the site where the Wade plane went down," Staff Sergeant Blankenship said as she placed some messages and letters on her desk.

"What did the General have to say about this and why wasn't I called at home?"

"Sir, the General said for you to come to his office after you have a cup of coffee this morning, and you weren't called at home because we weren't notified until after we showed for work."

"I see. Any idea when the civilian reported the beacon? I mean was it last night or the night before?"

"No, not really. Sir, we're looking into it right now and have phone calls out, but so far we've only got what the General told us."

"Well, I'm skipping the coffee and I'll be in the General's office if you need me."

"Yes, sir," She replied and went back to sorting her paperwork.

Turning, Wilcox made his way to the General's office and when he entered, his secretary smiled and said, "Go on in, he's expecting you."

The Colonel knocked once on the door, heard Moores command him to enter and walked in. The General had a big smile on his face as he said, "Have a seat, because after I tell you what's going on, you'll fall over if you don't.

"Yes sir," The Colonel replied and sat in a plush chair in front of the General's desk.

"Frank, last night a civilian pilot reported hearing a beacon on guard near where the Wade plane went down. He even talked to Sergeant Banks for a few seconds before he lost communications. Banks, thank God, reported he and David Wade were both alive and able to continue surviving. I think his words were, 'We're both fine and can continue on' or something like that. The Command Post has the exact wording from the pilot."

Leaning forward with a big smile on his face, Wilcox said, "That's great news!"

"Wait," General Moores replied, "It gets better. I contacted Rescue Headquarters at Scott and they gave me authorization for more missions."

"How many more, sir?"

The General laughed and replied, "Frank, we know exactly where they are, thanks to that pilot, so all we have to do is go in and bring them home."

Realizing what the General said was true, Wilcox stood and said, "Sir, if you will excuse me, I have a crew to notify and some work to do."

Chuckling, Moores replied, "I'd imagine you do. Let me know the minute they return!"

Saluting, the Colonel moved quickly from the General's office.

Once in his office he picked up the phone and called Cathy. After she answered, he said, "Cathy, a pilot talked to the P.J. that's with David last night and we're going out to bring them home."

"I'll be out at the base in a few minutes! Oh my God, my son is alive!"

"Cathy, please don't do that just yet. There are a lot of things that could go wrong right now, weather, aircraft and other things. Why don't you wait until I get confirmation from the rescue bird that David is onboard first?"

"Okay, I can do that, but do you think a problem might come up?"

"I'll be honest with you, I have no idea. But, I've learned in this business not to take anything for granted. The main reason I called was to let you know your son is alive and as of last night, healthy. I'll give you a call when I know more!"

CHAPTER 16

D avid was cold and the wind had a knife-like edge as he moved over the tundra. Vittles was walking in front and Banks was last in line. The P.J. was still upset that his radio had stopped working while he was talking to the pilot the night before. He knew it was the batteries, only there was nothing he could do. He'd wanted to tell the man in the plane he was moving to a small native village, only his radio stopped at the wrong time.

"David, are you hangin' tough?" Banks asked, knowing the young man must be tired. They'd been moving for hours.

"I'm okay, just sore is all."

"Keep your spirits up, the plane I spoke with last night will send a rescue bird our way at some point today!"

"But we moved since you talked."

"Yep, and we had to move. We would have frozen to death in the open like that. We need to find some trees and wait."

Vittles turned and said, "There's some nigh on five miles further along. They're growing right beside the river."

"We'll stop there. That will place us within ten miles of where we were last night, and we can wait for rescue there."

"It's snowing again!" David yelled out as he pointed at the flakes.

Turning to Vittles, Banks asked, "Is that all it does here, snow?"

Grinning, the old miner said, "Yup, but usually only from about September to May or so, although I've seen 'er snow in August before." Vittles then grinned at his joke.

"Let's move, because it's too cold to make small talk right now. My thermometer showed a temperature of minus fifteen a few minutes ago."

Moving forward, Vittles replied, "We've seen it colder. I can remember one year, it got so cold the bears were wearing parkas."

All laughed and then it became quiet as each thought of where they were and the chances of being rescued. Vittles wasn't worried much because he knew the land, Banks wanted his mission to be a success, and David just wanted to go home to his mother and sister.

* * *

Hours later, they walked into a small grove of trees lining the river. The forest was stunted and none of the trees was over seven feet tall, but with a shelter, it would offer protection from the wind.

Banks said, "David, I need you to find all the dead wood you can. You might have to break some off the trees. Usually the lower limbs will be the dead ones, if there are any on the tree."

"I'll get the shelter up, if one of ya'll get a fire goin'. I'm cold and it's pretty nippy out here," Vittles said as he pulled an old tarp from his backpack.

"I'll have one burning in a few minutes."

Banks quickly gathered tinder, kindling, and enough wood to make his fire and within minutes, the flames were flickering loudly. Vittles came to the fire, held his palms to the heat and smiled when he said, "Nothin' like a good fire to make a man feel like he ain't no caveman!"

Banks, looked around the area, and then said, "This is a good spot. We're in a long wide valley and if a plane fly's near us, I should be able to use the radio. Only, once the camp is established, we'll put some signals out too. Next aircraft I hear I want to take me home."

"We'll survive. Actually, other than the cold, we're pretty safe."

"Safe, yes, but not home."

Vittles shrugged his shoulders and replied, "Sooner or later, ya'll get back. The key is to stay alive until your chopper comes."

"I know we will, but I'll bet my wife is worried to death. The Air Force most likely terminated the search, which to them will mean I'm dead, but my wife won't believe I'm dead until she see's my body."

"Good woman ya have then."

Chuckling, Banks replied, "Yep, she really is, except I don't tell her often enough. Seems when you see a person day after day for years, some things go unsaid."

"After my wife died, I come to understand that part of our marriage. I always thought we had years left, only we didn't. Son, when you get home, be sure and tell your wife you love her. And, tell her every single day of your life after that."

Getting uncomfortable talking about his marriage and love, Banks called out to David as he approached with an armload of wood, "Bring the wood, and let's check our feet!"

"Our feet?" David asked as he dropped the wood near the fire.

"Yep, our feet, because the way we're moving our feet are taking a real beating. And, if our feet quit, we could be in serious trouble. Now, get your shoes and socks off so I can take a look at them, both of you."

Other than being red, Vittles' feet were in good shape, but he was wearing snow boots and they kept his feet very dry and warm. David's feet were white and skin was cracked around three of his toes. Banks saw they were bleeding little and looked as if he'd spent a long time in a bathtub.

"I was afraid this would happen when I gave you my wool socks. I think you have the beginning of immersion foot." He said.

David looked at his fish-belly colored feet and asked, "Is it bad? I won't lose my toes will I?"

"No, not at this stage. I need to dry them good, use some foot powder, and let you put on the other socks you have. You still have your old socks don't you?"

"Yep, I do. I'll put them on and then let these dry by the fire."

"Let's do your feet right now, because we can't take a chance with our feet," Banks replied and then pulled his medical bag to his side.

A few minutes later, David's feet were dry, coated with foot powder, and dry socks worn. He gave a big grin and said, "I didn't realize my feet were so cold, until you fixed them! Now they're as warm as toast!"

"Keep one pair of your socks dry at all times and when you feel your feet get damp, change them. Immersion foot can cause serious injury if your feet stay wet too long."

Vittles placed an old can they used to boil coffee in near the flames and added, "I saw this jasper once with trench foot so bad, the skin was a-comin' off in layers.

While I was dryin' his feet, they started to bleed and hurtin' 'em pretty bad."

Banks added a small log to the fire and then asked, "I'd imagine he didn't walk well for a few days, did he?"

"Nope, he hobbled around for almost two weeks on his feet a-fore he could walk without a limp. Nasty doin's, feet problems are."

"How come you called it trench foot and Sergeant Banks called it immersion foot? Aren't they the same?" David asked as he put his boots back on and laced them up.

"Yep, they're the same problem." Banks replied and then added, "During the First World War, thousands of men were fighting in trenches, and they usually had some water in the bottom of them. Doctors soon discovered if a man ignored his feet and they stayed wet, he eventually come down with immersion foot. But, in those days, the military called it trench foot, because that's where most cases of the injury came from, trenches. These same doctors discovered if a man kept his feet as dry as possible, used foot powder daily and changed socks when his feet were wet, the injury would almost go away."

"Almost?" David asked.

"Yep, almost. See, it was hard to completely prevent it, because no man alive could keep his feet completely dry all the time while living in a muddy trench for months. But, the severity of the injury could be greatly reduced through prevention."

There came a sudden gust of wind and snowflakes began to fall. The sky overhead was low thick looking white clouds, but not dark gray, so it looked to Banks to be an isolated snowfall.

"Angel One, Save One, do you copy?" His PRC-90 radio abruptly squawked.

Pulling the radio from his survival vest pocket, remembering he'd turned the radio on a few minutes earlier to monitor the fifteen minute call window. "Save One, read you five by five."

"John, this is Zee. Turn your radio on beeper and walk me to you, over."

"Roger, understand I am to go to beeper, wait one."

Banks moved the knob on his radio to beeper and listened as he heard the helicopter near. When he estimated the aircraft was heading right for him, he flipped the radio button to voice and said, "I hear you and am starting the count. Continue on your current heading."

"Roger, start the count, Angel One," Captain Zlotkowski replied.

"Ten. . . nine. . . eight. . . seven. . . six. . . five. . . four. . . three. . . two. . . one. . . . . . over. . . head, now!"

"Mark! Got your location!" Zee said and then a minute later added, "Cloud cover is too low to pick you up at this time, Angel One, but I have some early Christmas presents for you!"

"What about lowering the penetrator?"

"No can do, having problems with the winch. It worked fine at Elmendorf, but when we checked it a few minutes ago, nothing! Do you have any special needs at this time?"

Banks knew the question was Zee's way of asking if they were all okay and without serious medical problems. "Negative on the special needs, our condition is fine, but running low on food. Be advised there are three souls on the ground. I repeat, three on the ground. All are males, Michael, Alpha, Lima, Echo, Sierra."

"Copy, three males on the ground and you need food. I am dropping you two MA-1 raft kits. So, move a bit and let me know when you're in a safe position for the drop."

Turning to Vittles and David, Banks said, "Let's move about fifty meters east and watch as they drop the kits. They'll come as low as they can, go into a hover, and then shove them out of the open door. We have to move because the kits are very heavy and the last thing we need is an injury."

A few minutes later, Banks said over the radio, "We have moved fifty meters east. Drop the kits to the west of our camp. I repeat, drop to the west of camp."

"Copy, Angel One, drop west of your position. Keep your heads down, we're dropping the kits in three seconds, 3. . . 2. . . 1, kits are out of the aircraft!"

Two large yellow containers fell from the clouds and struck the snow with a loud *thud*. Banks smiled when he saw they landed about fifty feet from their camp.

"Save One, Angel One, the kits are on the ground."

"Roger on the kits. Angel One, we have an abort due to weather. Rescue Center requests you remain at your present location, so the next time I can give y'all a ride home."

"Copy and we'll remain here, unless we have a sound reason to move. If we move, be advised it will be down river, toward the native village. Confirm you copy, Save One."

"Copy, you'll remain in place unless forced to move. Any future movement will be down river toward the village."

"Affirmative, Save One. You have a good day now and hope you're able to play taxi again soon."

Banks heard Zee laugh and then reply, "John, I'll try to pick you up tomorrow or as soon as the weather will allow. If you have an emergency, use guard to contact someone and have the information relayed to the Command Post."

171

"Understand, and will do. Have a safe flight back."

"Take care and stay safe until I get back. Save One, out."

"Angel One, out," Banks replied, grinned and said, "Okay, let's get one of those kits opened and see the goodies inside! We'll save the other one for later, if we need it."

"How do we open one of these things?" David asked.

"With care, because each has a twenty person life raft inside and it inflates automatically. While we don't need the raft, there is enough food, water, signaling gear, more radios and other stuff that will come in handy as we wait."

"MRE's?" The young man asked in excitement, because he loved them.

"Nope, afraid not, usually. Most likely we'll have some compressed high energy bars, hard chocolate, coffee, teas, sugar and some other small stuff. I'm more interested in the survival gear and signaling stuff. Now, it's possible the Life Support folks packed these kits special for us and if they did, we'll have a few surprises."

"Like what?"

"Who knows, but it will be stuff we need to survive with. Now, I'm not going to inflate the raft, so when I pull these snaps loose, help me roll the raft out. Once we have the raft out flat, we'll see the equipment bag." Banks said as he pulled the snaps and then grinned as he added, "Ok, now, let's get this done."

Ten minutes later the raft was as flat as a pancake and the yellow equipment container was sitting in the middle. Banks picked it up and moved to the shelter of the trees. As he walked, he said, "Vittles, if you would place some snow blocks around the edges of the raft, it'll make a pretty good signal. It's bright yellow, so if we can keep falling snow off of it, it'll help when they return."

"I can do that, and I think that's a dandy idea." The old trapper replied and then moved to start cutting snow blocks.

David added more wood to the almost dead fire and grew excited when Banks lowered the big bag to the snow, and then unzipped the container. Kneeling beside the bag, he pulled out three sleeping bags, a small stove like he had along with a case of fuel, a large box of MRE's, a dozen can's of water, an emergency strobe light, two radios with a box of extra batteries, two knives, casualty blankets, and a lot more. Looking at it all, the P.J. said, "Life Support packed this special for us, because it's not configured like a normal kit. There are even long underwear and hats in this bag."

"How many meals are in the MRE box?" David asked as he leaned forward.

Placing the box in front of David, Banks chuckled and said, "Count them and see. I'm sure there are enough until we are rescued."

A few minutes later, the young man said, "Forty-five and that's enough for us to each eat three meals a day, for five days! And, we still have more in the other kit too!"

Handing David four sea marker dyes, Banks said, "This stuff is used to change the water around a lifer aft to florescent green, but later we can take it out by the raft and sprinkle it over as much snow as possible. This dye, along with the yellow raft, will make it easier to see us when they come back."

"Cool!" David replied as he took the containers and made his way to the fire.

Later that night, over supper, Banks looked at David and said, "You can have any two of the MRE's tonight. I know you like them, and I expect our ride home to return any day now."

"The snow will have to slow down a might first, don't ya think?" Vittles asked as he picked up a MRE and dropped it in a large can of boiling water."

"Yep, it's not safe with us in the trees and them wanting to rescue us. The aircraft commander was smart not to attempt it. In a war, they would have come down, but they don't need to do that for us. We're in no real danger and it's just not worth the risk in lives."

"Well, it might snow like this for a week, so we'll have to go easy on the rations after today." David stated and then dropped his MRE's in the water beside the other one.

Vittles gave him a light pat on the shoulder as he said, "A young jasper like ya needs more food than me or John."

"He's right though. These rations have a high calorie count, so there is no need to eat more than one a meal at a time. I gave the extra one to David tonight because it's been a long time since he's had a good hot meal," Banks replied and then winked at Vittles.

With a fake look of shock on his face, the old trapper asked, "What! Ya don't think my cookin' is a good meal?"

Everyone laughed and it felt good.

CHAPTER 17

"Wade residence, Cathy speaking," Cathy said as she answered the phone. She'd been preparing dinner and thinking of her son. She prayed it wasn't a telemarketer or she'd turn rude. She was in no mood to be bothered right now.

"Cathy, Frank Wilcox, here. I have some wonderful news for you."

"What do you have? Did David return with the crew?" She asked as her heart began to pound with excitement.

"Zee and his crew tried to rescue David today. When they neared the location, they found the whole area socked in with low clouds. They were even in radio contact with our P.J. on the ground and he informed them that all goes well. Now, normally, they would have lowered a stokes litter or a forest pen-etrator for an extraction, but the winch didn't work. We left them with enough food and gear to survive almost two weeks, but I'm sure the weather will break before then."

"They couldn't land?"

"Zee wanted to land, but I refused to give him permission. According to our maps, they are beside a river and it has a grove of trees near. My concern was a rotor blade would strike a tree. I couldn't take the risk of losing a crew. I'm sorry."

"Frank, it's alright, I just wondered. No, don't risk the lives of your men, especially when David is fine. They are both well, aren't they?"

"They told the pilot they picked up another man, but I don't know where that could have happened, unless they met a native or a trapper out there. They also have no special needs and that means to us they have no medical emergencies. All they requested was more food, which we dropped to them. Cathy, I'm very sure they are all well, warm, and now have enough food that we can relax a little."

"Any ideas when they might be able to come home?"

"The weather shop is working that issue for me, along with the Chaplin. First break in the weather and we'll go in again. I promise you. And, when this is all said and done, remember your David is one smart and brave boy!"

"He's like his father," Cathy replied and then fought back tears.

"Well, I've got to run and see the General, but I'll give you a call as soon as I learn something. I'm glad you didn't make the trip out earlier to meet them. It would have been a wasted trip."

"I don't see it that way. Oh, once this is all over, I want to have your crews over for a meal."

Laughing, Wilcox replied, "Watch my boys then, they all love food. I'll see you later Cathy and if you need anything give Carol a call."

"Bye," Cathy said and as she placed the phone back on the charger, she prayed, "Please God, let them get to David quickly. I never realized what I had, until you took part of it away from me. This I ask in the name of Jesus, amen."

David awoke a little after midnight and wondered why. Something must have aroused him. He listened, but heard nothing. He raised his head and near the dying fire, he saw a small animal licking the MRE pouches. Hoping to scare the animal away, he stood and moved near.

"Scat!" He said as he walked forward.

The animal was a little bigger than a fat tomcat and in the poor light he was unsure what it was. Probably just a raccoon, he thought as he kicked his foot at the animal's rear. Instead of running, the creature turned on him and when he got a glimpse of its face, David knew it was a badger. Sharp and long teeth punctured David's right boot and he felt pain. Before he could move, the animal had his legs and claws wrapped around the young man's leg.

Pain radiated up his leg and growing terrified, he screamed for help.

Banks, moving quickly, picked up David's rifle, placed the barrel against the small animals head and pulled the trigger. The sound of the shot was loud, but the badger immediately stopped moving—dead.

"It isn't dropping off of me!" The young man cried out in fear, "It's still alive!"

Vittles moved forward and began to peel the dead animals legs and teeth from David's leg he said, "Badgers never let go after they get a hold good. He's a gone goose, but he's got ya in a death grip."

"You sure he's dead?"

"Yup, as dead as last year's Christmas turkey," Vittles replied and then pulled the last claw from David's leg. Picking the dead animal up, the old miner walked into the darkness to get rid of the body.

Banks, who'd been waiting for Vittles to finish, now said, "Let's build this fire up and take a look at your injuries." He added three logs to the dying flames and continued, "Pull that leg up and let me take a good look at it."

The injuries on his leg were bleeding freely as Banks asked, "Your boot is torn, did he get your foot, too?"

"I think he attacked my foot first."

Banks unlaced the boot, removed a bloody sock and said, "Puncture wounds, and they're not easy to clean or treat. The injuries to your leg are mostly rips, tears, and a few bites."

David, who'd been thinking, suddenly asked, "What about rabies?"

"That's another concern I have right now, but we're putting the cart before the horse. First, I need to clean these wounds, disinfect them, and wrap them up good. I don't have a thing in the kit for rabies, so we'll have to wait and see. Did the animal act strange or seem unusual?"

"No, not really. I was just shocked that something that small would attack a human!"

Vittles had walked up, so he said, "Badgers are known for their guts. They ain't scared of a blame thing, includin' Grizzlies. Attacking you was nothin' to the small guy, he was jus' defendin' his meal."

"Do you think it was rabid?" Banks asked, as he wrapped the foot in gauze.

"Not likely, but we cain't rule it out."

"Now, it's likely David, you'll come down with a fever and some aches. I can give you some acetaminophen for both, but that's it. While I have some morphine and codeine medications, they're only for very serious injuries."

"That acet-a-thing, what is it?"

"Sort of like aspirin, but it's not. You've had it before, I'm sure, when you had colds, fevers, or small aches."

"My dad gave me things in the past, but I never paid much attention to medicines."

"Now, every morning we'll change the bandages, put more antibiotic ointment on the wounds, and you'll be fine in a few days. The puncture wounds are the ones to watch. I tried to get some medication in the holes, only I'm not sure how well I did."

Vittles, sitting by the fire with his never smoked pipe between his teeth said, "And, ya need to stay off your feet a few days. If ya move too much, them wounds will start bleedin' again."

Turning to the old man, David pointed at his old pipe and asked, "Don't you ever smoke that thing?"

Pulling the pipe from his teeth, Vittles replied, "I used to smoke it all the time, then 'bout twenty years back I quit smokin'. Now I just like the feel of the stem between my teeth."

Banks handed David two white pills and said, "These are the pills I told you about. Take these and then get some rest. Vittles was right too, stay off your feet for a few days."

After David was asleep, the snow began to fall once more and Banks asked, "What do you think about that badger?"

"I don't think it was rabid, if that's what you're really asking. They're a moody critter in the best of times, and what it did tonight is normal behavior for the little beast."

"Sounds like David kicked a running chainsaw blade, doesn't it?"

Snickering, Vittles replied, "Yep, they're just like a chainsaw in a lot of ways. A few years back I found two skeletons. One was a grizzly bear and the other was a badger. Some of the remains of that badger were on the bears face, holding its mouth closed, but the bear in anger or fear had killed the little thing. It must have

179

happened years before, except the claws and teeth of the little critter were still buried deep in the bear's bones."

"What gives them enough guts to attack a full sized grizz like that?"

"I ain't got no idea, but the natives say there are only two things in the world to fear, one is an insane woman, and the other is a badger on a good day. I think they might have a point."

Banks laughed and said, "I have lots of medical training, only it's how to treat a gunshot wound, fix broken bones, deliver a baby, and many other things. I don't remember any in-depth training on rabies and I know there's nothing in my bag to treat it."

"Well, your job was mainly created to save downed aircrews in times of war, I'd imagine. And, I remember you tellin' us most rescues happen within 24 hours, so I'd suspect the need for rabies vaccine or training just ain't there."

"Overall you're right, except during peace time we fly civilian rescue missions. Even during wars, we'll fly rescues here in the states if needed. We're committed to saving lives, under all conditions and anywhere."

Grabbing the coffee can, Vittles said, "You're deserving of the call sign, Angel One then. It's a special job ya got, son, so don't ya ever forget it either."

Standing, Banks replied, "I'm off to my sleeping bag. It's only a couple of hours until first light, but I want to be up by then. You can never tell when our ride home might show up."

"Yup, I hear ya, and I don't want to miss the ride neither!" Vittles said and then giggled like a little schoolgirl.

Morning came with snow flying all around and the temperature way below zero. The shelter was cold, even with a blazing fire burning right outside the entrance. The sleeping bags were rated to minus twenty, so Banks knew they were in no danger of freezing to death.

After a quick MRE for breakfast, Banks changed the bandages on David and then said, "Some inflammation there, but nothing to worry about yet. The triple antibiotic cream I'm using should clear that up fairly quickly."

Vittles, who didn't put much faith in antibiotic ointments, said, "We'll know by mornin' if that cream works or not."

"Why so quiet, David?" Banks asked as he closed his medical bag.

"I woke up thinking we'd all go home today, but it's snowing to beat the band out there right now."

"You can be sure Zee and the rescue squadron are monitoring the weather. If they're given enough time to slip in here and out, they'll come. It all depends if the weather window stays open long enough. I mean, there isn't a real rush to get to us, we're pretty safe."

Vittles met his eyes and nodded his head in a questionable way toward David. Banks, sure all the young man had was a slight infection, nodded in return, except his was a confident nod.

The snow was piling up by the inches against the shelter and the wind hadn't died down at all, when Vittles pulled his small pocket Bible out and began reading. While not an overly religious man, he did believe in God and tried to be an honest man. He knew God had a hand in all he did, but like most people, he often got busy and didn't read his Bible as often as he felt he should have. Now, following the destruction of

181

his cabin, he felt a need to understand the Good Book better.

Abruptly the shelter gave a violent shake and the trapper raised his head and looked around. David was curled up in his sleeping bag sleeping, Banks was going through the supplies, and he saw the shelter was in no danger of collapsing. Seeing things were normal, he lowered his eyes and began reading once again.

"Do you read the Bible much?" Banks asked as he closed his equipment bag.

"Not as much as I should, I guess."

"Hard to have religion out here in the bush, isn't it? I mean, where would you go to church?"

Vittles laughed and replied, "Son, I live in God's own church. I'm surrounded by beauty and a person can actually feel God out here. As for religion, no, it's not hard to have religion in the bush. I think it might even be easier, because I could look out a window of my cabin and see the results of God's mighty hand in the country around me. Now, if you mean a church and religion like you have in a town or city, I don't have that."

"Then how can you practice God's word?"

"I don't *practice* His word, I try to live it. See, I say a silent prayer when I get up and before I go to bed. All day long when I trap or look for gold, I see God's hand in the mountains, tundra, rivers and lakes. This country is jus' too pretty to have been created by accident or by nature. No, I have no problems being a Christian here."

"But you don't have a church, not a real one anyway."

"Before you two arrived, I'd spend my Sundays with God."

Confused, Banks asked, "How could you do that?"

Vittles laughed. "I'd get up early, clean up, shave, dress in my best clothes, and then listen to an early Baptist church service on the radio. After that was finished, I'd eat lunch and pray a spell on my own. I'd do no work, because it is a day of rest, so I'd read my Bible a bit and then listen to the afternoon services on my radio. After supper, I'd listen to the radio services again and just before bed I'd pray some more. I might lack other folks, but a man with a radio is never really alone."

"Then why did you stop when we arrived?"

"I stopped out of respect for the two of you. See, I had no idea of your beliefs and maybe it was wrong for me to stop, but I didn't want to seem to be pushing my God on you."

Banks laughed and said, "I am a regular church goer, so your Sunday church routine would not have bothered me and I would have joined you. My family is a member of a small Baptist church in Anchorage."

"I'm glad to hear that, John. I don't push religion, although I guess I should, but I try to respect the beliefs of others. I spent a couple of years in the military, and it taught me that other folks don't always share my beliefs in many areas, not just religion. So, usually I just stay quiet."

"Yep, I know exactly what you mean about the military. When I was in training, I was called Deacon, because of my strong religious views. I didn't mind, and as you know, everyone in the service has a nick-name or two anyway."

"Uh-huh, and mine was Fat Boy. I was overweight when I joined and my Drill Instructor immediately pinned the name on me. He'd yell for Fat Boy, and I always knew he meant me. But, I went to Vietnam weighing 180 pounds and when I returned a year later,

I weighed 120. I'd lost sixty pound through sweat and poor food."

Laughing, Banks replied, "And now you're as skinny as a beanpole split three ways."

"Some jaspers gain weight in middle age, I lost it. But, I think moving out to the bush dropped most of my pounds."

"Less fat in your diet?"

"Well, wild game is mostly lean, but I think it had to do with my new life. I walked countless miles a day looking for pelts or gold, so I got a lot of exercise. I no longer sit behind a desk on my butt and drink coffee all day long."

Banks nodded and said, "I'm usually up by four to do my daily five mile run. I then eat a light breakfast, usually just oatmeal and toast, and then go into work. My days are normally ten to twelve hours, so I'm a busy man all day. Most of the time we train hard, but there are situations like this where I earn my keep."

"Son, ya've more than earned your keep with us. Oh, I think David would have found his way to my cabin without ya, but I think he'd had some frostbite on 'em."

Looking over at the sleeping David, Banks said, "He's a smart young man and he's done very well out here. I think if he'd not been who he is, I would have found him dead."

"Good point, and I think you're right. I never knew his pa, but he must have been a good father. Boys don't turn into good men, unless a strong man is behind them durin' their early years."

Standing, Banks said, "I'm going to clear the snow off of the raft and listen on the radio for a few minutes. I'll not be gone long and when I come back we'll heat up some fresh coffee."

"It's still snowing hard and won't be light fer hours yet!"

"Uh-huh, it is, but the snow should be kept off that raft as much as possible. You and me both know the snow can stop in a heartbeat and if it does, the chopper might be back out."

"Ya go do that then, while I put the coffee on."

CHAPTER 18

"Angel One, this is Panama Two Niner, do you read me, over?" A female voice said over the radio as Banks removed it from his pocket.

"Roger, Panama Two Niner, go ahead."

"I'm a C-130 trash hauler on my way to Elmendorf and was asked to touch base with you if I could."

"I understand Panama Two Niner, and I have a slight problem here," Banks said and decided it was a good time to bring up David and the badger.

"What is the nature of your problem Angel One?"

"Contact the command post and inform them Wade, that's whiskey, alpha, delta, echo, has a foot and leg mauled by a badger. His condition is stable and not life threatening. I repeat, it is not life threatening. I need to know of any rabies in the area and possible treatment steps. Right now I'm treating it as an animal bite, over."

"Copy, Angel One. Wait one." The unknown woman said.

Banks knew the pilot would radio Elmendorf for the information and as soon as she got an answer she'd let him know.

"Angel One, Panama Two Niner." She said a few minutes later.

"Go, Panama Two."

"Negative on the rabies, there have been no known cases reported. The flight surgeon suggests you continue treating it as you are but watch for infection."

"Copy, no rabies and continue current treatment."

"Affirmative, Angel One. Elmendorf wants a situation report if possible."

"All are fine and in good health other than the Wade injury, nothing new to report at this time. We have plenty of food, water and clothing, over."

"I understand all is well."

"Roger that, all is well."

"Angel One, Elmendorf also said they will make another attempt as soon as the weather breaks."

"Thanks for the information, Panama Two Niner," Banks replied and then noticed the signal was getting weaker.

"Say again, Angel One, you're coming in broken."

"Thanks!"

"Angel One, Angel One, this is Panama Two   ."

I've lost the signal, must be my batteries! Banks thought, *it must be twenty below out here.*

Placing his radio in his pocket, he made his way to the shelter and entered. While he warmed by the fire he said, "I just spoke to a C-130 going to Elmendorf and the pilot checked on rabies information."

"Good news?"

"Uh-huh, I'd say so. There have been no reports of rabies in this area and the flight surgeon agreed with my treatment."

Putting his Bible in his shirt pocket, Vittles asked, "Did they say anything about a rescue attempt?"

Smiling Banks replied, "Yes they did. According to what was relayed to me, as soon as the weather breaks, they're coming."

"Now, that's excellent news!"

"We'll get out of this yet; we just need to be patient."

"Oh, I know that. I'm just gettin' tired of sleeping in a bag at night and not bein' able to listen to my radio."

"I'd appreciate a good hot meal, followed by an even hotter shower."

"Yep, we're all a little gamey right now."

"I'm more worried about how David will react to the death of his father once back home than anything else right now. Not many kids get to watch a parent die right before their eyes, and especially in a situation like he did. I'm wondering how badly it frightened him."

"It'll affect him for life and we both know that, but exactly how much is hard to tell. I only know Doctor Wade died, but David knows how well he died."

Leaning toward the fire, Banks asked, "What does that mean?"

"Well, if the man died a hard painful death, he might have screamed a lot or cried for help. On the other hand, if he took his death in a more peaceful way, it won't hurt David as much, maybe. I ain't no shrink, but people tend to remember screams for pain and help. See, during the war, I saw lots of men die and in many different ways. I remember those that died hard, but not a one of those that died easy."

"I see. David is a strong lad and I hope his father's death was a quiet one. He said he was with his dad when he died, so it will have some impact on his mind. I think, when we get back, I'll suggest to his mother to have him see a psychologist a few times."

Vittles thought for a minute or two and then said, "I'd talk to the boy first. Some folks don't cotton much to head doctors."

"Oh, I'll do that as well. Most folks get over the physical trauma of a survival situation fast once back

189

home, but the mental aspect takes a long time. This is especially true if there have been deaths."

"Look, survival ain't much different than fightin' in a war. In both cases, a person is fightin' for their lives. Some survive and some don't. That causes survivors guilt, or so I read once."

"You mean the old, why did I survive and my friends didn't guilt trip?"

"Uh-huh and from what I read, soldiers often have it."

"I can tell you right now why David survived. He was lucky enough to survive the crash without serious injury, while his father wasn't, and he did almost everything right after that. Sure, he burnt his shelter down, but he didn't give up, while a lot of other folks would have. Of all his strengths, he has a strong will to survive."

* * *

Colonel Wilcox drove to the Wade house and knocked on the door. When Cathy opened it, he smiled and said, "I have some additional information."

"You're smiling, so it must be good news then." She replied as she motioned for him to enter.

"Well, some of it is excellent and the rest is maybe bad, but it depends on your view."

Walking into the living room, Wilcox saw Marie sitting on the sofa watching television.

"Have a seat and let me know what you've got," Cathy said and felt her fear returning.

"First, your David had a bit of a run with a Badger, which he lost. According to the P.J. on the ground, one of David's legs is scratched and clawed up a little. He also suffered a few bites. Overall he's in good condition, but I'd suspect a little sore right now."

"What about rabies?"

"According to the base conservation department, there are no documented cases of rabies in the area, and never have been. We've kept records since the Second World War and not a thing has ever been recorded. That means our P.J. can most likely just treat him for puncture wounds and minor cuts and be done. Now, there is always the danger of infection, because badgers will eat almost anything and they're dirty.

"Frank, I'm a nurse, or did you forget?"

"No, just reminding you is all."

"Now, was that the good or bad news?"

"Bad, the good news is we'll have a five hour window the day after tomorrow to go in and bring our men home."

Cathy jumped to her feet, screamed and then said, "Oh, thank you, Jesus!"

Wilcox, a little embarrassed, lowered his eyes.

"And thank you and your men too, Frank! I'm so happy right now!" Then she suddenly quieted, sat back down, and asked in a low voice, "Do you think it will really happen?"

Shrugging, with his hands out, Wilcox replied, "Cathy, I'm going by what my weather boys told me, and I have the General's permission to launch the mission, so yes, I think it will really happen."

Marie asked, "What's a badger?"

"It's a cocky little critter, not much bigger than my house cat, which thinks he's the king of the woods. He'll attack anything, and I do mean anything. They've been seen attacking grizzlies, moose, and of course, humans. Small, but mean, too. I think David can tell you all about them in a couple of days."

"I don't think I ever want to see a real one!" Marie said, and then laughed.

191

"Your brother is okay, or Sergeant Banks would have reported otherwise. See, the P.J. has a lot of training in the medical field, so he's fully capable of treating any one of us. David is *almost* as safe with Banks as he would be with a doctor."

At the mention of a doctor, Cathy broke into tears.

"I'm sorry Cathy, I didn't mean to upset you."

"Frank, it's me, not you. I have to learn to accept the death of Jim, and that will take time."

"Smile for me, please, because we'll have Dave home soon and two days from now you'll have dinner with your boy."

Lowering her head, Cathy replied, "I hope so, but this has been a real roller coaster of a rescue."

"Some are like this, but very few. Usually we have the survivors out within 24 hours or so. It's the weather that has been holding us up."

Giving him a weak smile, she said, "I know and I'm not blaming you for a single thing. I appreciate all you, the Air Force, Civil Air Patrol, and FAA have done for me and my family."

Standing, Colonel Wilcox said, "It's our jobs, remember?"

"That others may live, right?" Marie said, gave a thumbs up, and then smiled.

* * *

"The leg looks bad to me," Vittles said from beside the fire. The night was very cold and Banks had told him it was fifty below zero.

There came a loud popping sound outside the shelter and David asked, "What was that noise?"

"Likely a limb just broke from the cold. If it gets too cold the moisture in tree limbs freeze and they can explode," the old trapper said with a grin.

"You're not serious!" David said with a frown on his face. He suspected the old trapper was pulling his leg.

"As serious as I can be. Things start to change in weather this cold. Right now, if we were out, any exposed flesh would freeze in under a minute."

Banks, speaking as he opened his medical bag said, "What he's saying is true, David. Weather like this is a real killer. Be thankful we have a fire, shelter, and sleeping bags. If not, we'd have a rough night of it, with no promise it would be warmer in the morning."

"Why do you have a needle in your hand?"

"Dave, your injury has an infection, and I need to give you a shot of penicillin. Do you know if you're allergic to any drugs or anything else?" Banks asked and then pushed the plunger just enough to rid the syringe of air.

"Not that I know of, and I'm sure dad would have said something about it if I was."

"Okay, I need for you to lower your pants and roll over on your belly."

"What! I'll do no such thing."

Banks and Vittles laughed hard. After a few minutes, Banks said, "David, as cold as this medicine is, I have to give it to you in your rear. Besides, that's where a doctor would give it to you anyway. If we don't treat this with antibiotics, you'll only get worse."

"I'll do it, but I don't like it!" David said as he unbuckled his belt, unzipped his pants, and then rolled over.

"Good and I'll remember you don't like this!" Banks replied and then grinned at the young man's spunk.

"Ooowww, that stings!"

"Beats dying of infection, doesn't it?"

"Yea, but you didn't say anything about it hurting."

"You can roll back over and pull your pants back up now. The sting is slight and knowing you're a man, well, I didn't see a need to warn you."

Redressing, David asked, "How long will the lump be in my rear?"

"Until the medicine warms a little more and is absorbed by your body."

"I hope it's soon, because my leg really hurts."

"I have another pain killer I can give you, but I won't give it to you until later today. It can lead to addiction and I don't like using it."

"I can survive until later, because my dad warned me about drugs."

"The use of drugs is fine, as long as they are not abused. Just follow your doctor's orders and you're safe enough, most of the time. The key to safe drug use is talking to your physician on a regular basis."

"Ya got some opiate based drugs?" Vittles asked.

"Yep, codeine, and it works for moderate to serious pain. I just don't like using them if it can be avoided."

"From the look of his leg, it has to hurt 'em some. I'm sure he won't turn into a junky over the next few days. Although I did see drugs abused in Vietnam a few times."

Banks laughed and replied, "I'll give him some near bed time to ease the pain, so he can get some sleep tonight. And, we're not in a war zone. Now, you and I have to go out into this storm and gather some more wood."

Two days later, Zee and his crew lifted off from Elmendorf with the ambient air temperature minus forty. The sky was a clear blue and the trees were covered in frost as the chopper moved toward the rescue point.

Nearing the site Zee said, "As cold as it is, I want Williams to go down the hoist and help bring them up, if need be. Hopefully I can land and then bring them aboard."

Staff Sergeant Williams replied, "Copy, sir."

"With this weather like it is, make sure they're bundled up good for the ride up if we have to use the winch."

"I got a beeper on guard." Captain Baldwin said in a casual voice.

"Radio on guard frequency, this is Save One, do you require assistance?" Zee asked after he keyed his microphone.

"Roger that, this is Angel One, and I need a ride home."

"Angel One, we are ten mikes from your location, over."

"Copy Save, I have you visual."

"I see a large yellow panel of some sort."

"We are fifty feet to the west of that marker. It's the raft, so keep it in mind if you land."

"Understand you are fifty feet west of the marker. John, move your people from the shelter and position them to your east. Make it about a hundred meters from your camp."

"Will do, Save."

Turning, Banks called out, "Grab your coats and what gear you want to take home and let's move!"

Vittles and David were soon standing beside Banks as the chopper approached. Smiling, David asked, "What now?"

"We need to move a hundred meters east and wait. Once the bird lands we can board." Then speaking into the radio he asked, "Save One, are you sending a P.J. out?"

"Affirmative on the P.J.."

"Okay," Banks added, "When the P.J. exits the aircraft, we'll go back with him one at a time. David, since you're injured I want you to go first, then Vittles, and last will be me. Now, let's move out a ways."

"Angel One, this is Save One, do you have smoke?"

"Roger on the smoke. I am popping it now!" Banks pulled the lanyard on his MK-13 Mod-O flare and a thick orange smoke filled the air.

"Why the smoke?" Vittles asked.

"So the pilot can see wind direction and land into the wind."

"Cool," David said, "That's smart!"

Banks laughed and watched the chopper as it lowered slowly toward the ground. He used both arms to signal the pilot from the air to the snow. It seemed to take it forever, but he knew it was because he was cold, tired and hungry.

"Angel One, I'm on the ground. Willie will be out for you in a few seconds."

"Remember, we go back to the bird one at a time. I don't need any confusion and here comes Willie right now," Banks reminded the two survivors.

The man approaching wore his dark visor down on his helmet and hunched over as he walked under the big rotating blades of the helicopter. When he neared he asked, "Can all of you walk?"

Banks replied, "We're fine Willy, but take Wade first, he's been injured slightly." Then extending his hand, he and Staff Sergeant "Willie" Williams shook hands.

Within a few minutes, the survivors were loaded, strapped in, and the chopper was rising from the frozen tundra. When the aircraft had gained about a hundred feet of height, Williams handed each of them a hot cup of coffee. Smiling, he gave a thumbs up and all three returned the sign quickly.

In the cockpit, Zee was speaking to the command post, "Roger, we have the survivors and are returning to base."

The pilot then heard Colonel Wilcox ask, "Understand you have all three, is that correct Save One?"

"That's a big Roger, colonel, all three, so I'd suggest you give this boys mom a call, sir!"

"Well done, Save One, very well done."

"We're coming home, Save One out."

CHAPTER 19

The aircraft made too much noise for any of them to speak without a headset, so the three survivors sat quietly with their eyes closed. All were cold, David was excited, Vittles was worried about the loss of his cabin, and Banks felt satisfied. He'd done what needed to be done, and overall, he found no fault in his actions. Every few minutes, Williams would appear and see if they needed more coffee or anything else during the flight. While each was shivering, though wrapped in thick wool blankets, David knew his body temperature was low and he was very likely dehydrated. Knowing this, he still drank cup after cup of the steaming hot coffee. Banks had warned him earlier not drink too much coffee, because the caffeine only made dehydration worse, but David was so cold his hands shook.

An hour after liftoff from the tundra, Williams appeared and said in almost a scream, "In five minutes we'll land. Wait for my instructions before you leave the aircraft. Each of you will visit the hospital first. Nod if you understand me!"

All nodded, and then suddenly David felt fear gnawing at his stomach. He'd be facing his mother and now he had to tell her dad was dead. Oh, he was aware she knew, but it was something he had to tell her himself.

The chopper stood still in the air for a minute or two and then slowly began to lower to the ground. From the window in the side door, David could see two ambulances and scores of people, including the press. He grew more concerned when he heard the aircraft touch ground. A few minutes later the engines began to give a different pitch, so he knew the aircraft engines were shut down.

Hands reached in and helped the three to waiting ambulances as a military representative said to the news crews, "The survivors are being taken to the hospital for routine medical evaluations. Following the evaluations, the United States Air Force will hold an official press conference in the medical facility."

Once in the ambulance, David was strapped to a gurney and the man beside him said, "I am Technical Sergeant Lopez, and if you need anything during the short ride, let me know."

"I'm fine, but when will I see my mother?"

"She was at the hospital the last time I saw her, with Colonel Wilcox. But, it might be an hour or so before she's allowed to see you. The doctor wants to give you a good going over before you have any visitors."

Nodding, David closed his eyes and relaxed. He was finally home. Then he thought, *Dad, I made it! I want you to know, I didn't give up! I love you, Dad!*

The medical technician saw the tears on David's face, but never knew the reason.

Two hours later, as he rested in a hospital bed, his mother entered the room with Colonel Wilcox. She ran to his bedside and held him closely, not saying a word. Finally, after about five minutes, David said, "Mom, look at me. I have something to say to you."

She broke her hug, looked into her son's eyes as he said, "I was with Dad when he died. He was a brave man, mom, and while in pain, he kept telling me how to survive."

Cathy gave a cry of anguish, threw her arms around her son and said, "Let's not talk about your father right now. I'm so thankful to have you home!"

Seeing Colonel Wilcox, David said, "Thank you for bringing me home, sir."

The Colonel extended his hand and said as they shook, "Welcome home, David. We got to you as soon as we could."

"I know you did and Sergeant Banks deserves a medal for what he did for us."

"We're well aware of the performance of Sergeant Banks, and he'll have his medal."

At that point, a flight surgeon entered the room and asked, "David, other than your badger marks, you're in great shape. I understand Sergeant Banks gave you some penicillin for the infection, so I'll give you some pills to take at home. As far as I'm concerned, you can leave now, if you want."

His mom was still hugging him, so David said, "Mom, did you hear the doctor? I can go home now. Mom?"

Smiling, the Colonel said, "Give her a few more minutes, David, she thought she'd lost both of you."

Kissing her on the forehead, David said, "I'm home now, mom, and I love you."

* * *

A week after returning, David was the guest on a nationwide talk show. He was nervous and sat between his mother and sister.

The director raised three fingers and then lowered them one at a time. Finally, he pointed at the show's host.

"Good morning, I'm George Burton and welcome to Your News This Morning. We have a special guest with us today, David Wade, who survived weeks in some of the roughest country in the world—the frozen wilderness of Alaska. David is a young man who survived a bear attack, temperatures as low as minus fifty, and who walked miles over frozen tundra. Good morning David."

"Good morning."

"David, at any time during your situation did you ever feel like giving up?"

"I felt like giving up every single day, and it was hard, especially after my dad died. I would have given up, but my father taught me determination when it came to survival. He called it the will to survive.

"Why didn't you give up, David?"

"I promised my dad I'd live and it was a promise I had to keep. I called on God when I felt really low." David said, as his eyes watered, and then added, "My father was a very special man and when he died he was more worried about me than himself. How many folks would be like that? Don't you see, I had to live for my dad."

"He sounds like a very courageous man, and you're a lot like him, I might add."

Wiping his eyes, David replied, "I hope I'm one tenth the man my father was."

Marie was sitting quietly when the show's host turned to her and asked, "Marie, how did you feel when you discovered your brother was alone and your father dead?"

Marie blinked a few times and then said, "I don't mean to be rude, but what kind of a dumb question is

202

that? How do you think I felt? You remind me of a report I once saw on TV where a woman lost her whole family in a house fire. The reporter had the nerve to ask her, 'How do you feel?' Are all reporters stupid, or just some of you?"

Taken back by the sudden attack, the host blushed and quickly said, "Well, perhaps you took my question in a negative way. I meant would you explain your feelings for our viewers."

David and his mother exchanged grins, knowing little Marie had just put the reporter in his place.

"David and I are normal kids, and that means we fight at times. I love my brother and I'm very proud of him. I respect him a great deal now, knowing he survived all alone on a mountain. Like anyone who loves another person, I was frightened he might die alone on some snowy clump of rock, not knowing I loved him."

"Does that mean you'll no longer fight?"

Marie laughed and replied, "I suspect we'll still fight at times, but not over little things like we once did. Didn't you fight with your brothers and sisters?"

"Huh?"

"I asked if you fought with your siblings."

"Of course I didn't I was an only child."

Marie smiled and replied, "I'm sure you were."

* * *

Later, back home, David began to do the things he'd always done, and for some reason they didn't excite him as they once had. He missed his Dad and while he talked about his feelings with his mother, he had refused to see anyone associated with the mental health field.

A month after the rescue, Sergeant Banks arrived at the door and when he entered, he saw David sitting at the kitchen table. Smiling he said, "David, I'm getting a couple of medals tomorrow and wondered if you would attend. I have a surprise for you once it's over."

"Sure, we'll come, won't we, mom?"

Cathy started to say no, but changed her mind because Banks had done so much for her son. Smiling, she said, "We wouldn't miss it for anything. What time and where?"

"Fourteen hundred, uh, I mean, two in the afternoon, at the Search and Rescue Squadron."

Laughing, Cathy said, "John, I know military time. I've been around Elmendorf all of my life. If nothing else has rubbed off, military time has."

"Well," Banks said embarrassed, "My wife and I would love to see you there." Then turning to David he added, "Wear something nice for me, it's a special day."

* * *

At fourteen hundred hours, David and his family were sitting in a big meeting room when a Senior Master Sergeant, with a sleeve full of stripes, stepped in and yelled, "Ten-hut!"

Men and women stood at attention as Colonel Wilcox entered and said, "Be seated." He moved to the podium and cleared his throat, before saying, "We are here today to honor men of our own. It gives me extreme personal pleasure in recognizing five men this afternoon for their actions in the Wade rescue." At that point, Zee and his crew, along with Sergeant Banks walked in, one behind the other, and stood facing the audience. Each of Zee's crew was presented medals individually and citations were read for each man. Finally, Colonel Wilcox moved to Banks and stood at attention as a narrator read three citations. At the end of each reading, the Colonel would pin the medal to his left chest and then shake his hand. When the ceremony was over for Banks, he wore an Air Medal, Humanitarian Service Medal, and an Airman's Medal. He'd also been promised his next performance report would be endorsed by both General Moores and the PACAF commander.

Turning to face the audience, the Colonel grinned and said, "Now, because we had a left over stripe on base, Sergeant Banks is now Staff Sergeant Banks." He handed a set of stripes to the surprised Sergeant and said, "Well done, John."

Returning to the podium, Colonel Wilcox said, "Staff Sergeant Banks now has a special presentation he'd like to do. John, if you'll come up here, I'll turn this show over to you."

Banks walked to the microphone and said, "As most of you know, training to be in pararescue is hard, and many of the people who try out don't have what it takes." Then, pulling a sheet of paper from his uniform blouse, he continued with, "Mister David Wade, would you come forward, please."

David made his way to the front of the room and stood looking at the group. He saw grizzled old Sergeants with more stripes than a zebra and lots of officers. He suddenly felt nervous.

"This young man survived in the arctic all alone for many long and cold days. He lived on a mountain, following the death of his father, and faced temperatures as low as minus fifty. He made his own shelter, gathered his own water, and even procured his own food. Then, seeing smoke in the distance, he walked for many miles over open tundra toward that smoke, and his only chance for survival. The temperature, ladies and gentlemen, was an average of minus twenty, and he did it for days! David did something that many of us in this room could not have done. He survived an extremely hostile environment to live another day, and it is with great pleasure I award him the position of an honorary P.J. in the United States Air Force, along with an honorary enlisted rank of Sergeant."

Stepping forward, Banks picked up a maroon beret, with the distinguished emblem of a pararescueman on the front. Placing it on David's head, he saluted him, and then said, "Always remember this moment and keep in mind our motto."

"That others may live." David replied with a serious tone.

There came a loud round of yelling, clapping and catcalls, before Banks raised his hands and said, "That concludes my award, but I invite all of you to stay a while and enjoy the punch and pastries."

Moving to David's side a little later, Banks said, "You deserve the honor you received today, David."

An older man moved forward, cracked a big tooth-gapped grin and said, "By golly, I was proud of ya both!"

"Vittles!" David cried, and moved to hug the man.

"Easy son, ya cain't hug me like yer doin' fer long, I'm an old man, remember?"

Laughing, David replied, "I'm surprised, first the beret and now you!"

"Ya didn't think I'd forget two special men now, did ya?"

Banks laughed and said, "Let's mingle with the crowd a little, David, and then we'll all three go out for a drink or burger."

A little later, as the three of them sat in the Base Exchange Mall, sipping on ice cold drinks, David looked over at Vittles and asked, "Did you find a place to stay for a while?"

"Yup, I did. I've decided it's time for me to live in town fer a spell. I fig'ered at my age, it would be smarter for me to live around folks than away from them. I'm too old to be living like I was in the bush."

"Will you be happy doing this?" Banks asked.

"I think so. I found me a good church, nice apartment, and even met me a woman."

"Good luck on all three and I'm glad you're doing so well."

"Aren't you?"

Banks grinned and said, "I'm about to be a father!"

"Well, I'll be doggone, our Sergeant Banks will be a pa-pa!"

David grinned and asked, "Doesn't it scare you to know you'll soon be a father? It would me."

Growing serious, Banks replied, "No, I'm not really scared, but I'm concerned. You know, I jump out of airplanes and that doesn't worry me as much as the thought of being a daddy."

"Yep, the little critters don't come with no owner's manual or nothin'. The Good Lord drops just them in the middle of our laps and we're left to do the best job we can on our own."

"John, you'll make a good father and I know it," David said and then smiled.

"How can you know that?"

"Because you're cut from the same cloth my father was. He was a strong man, just like you are. He was tender when he needed to be, a teacher to me and my sister, and a fair but strict disciplinarian when it called for it. I'm lucky to have had him in my life, especially when I was alive and alone on a mountain."

THE END

Glossary

360: When an aircraft flies 360 degrees, or a circle. Often done when waiting for further instructions, to burn fuel on purpose, or preparing to land.

Abort: To cancel or call off the flight of an aircraft

AC: Aircraft Commander, the pilot

AO: Area of operations

Assistant Team Leader: The number two man in charge of a team of military men.

Band-aid: Often a radio call sign for a medic

BDU: Camouflage field uniform used by military personnel

Bingo on fuel: Running out or low on aircraft fuel.

Bird: Helicopters or any aircraft

Blood trail: A trail of blood left by a person who has been injured

Body bag: Plastic or rubber bag used to transport dead bodies from crash sites

Bush: Military term for the field (woods, mountains, and so on)

Chinook: CH-47 cargo helicopter

Chopper: A slang name for a helicopter

Copy: I understand, hear you, know what you mean, etc... an acknowledgment of understanding.

Countdown: Used by the survivor to indicate to a rescue aircraft when they fly overhead. Used mostly in areas with limited visibility and is an actual countdown starting with any number, but when the aircraft is overhead, the survivor says, "Overhead now!"

CP: Command Post

Doc: Medic, corpsman, or doctor

D-ring: A D-shaped metal snap link used to hold gear together and used in rappelling from choppers.

Dust-off: Medical evacuation by helicopter

EM: Enlisted man

ETA: Estimated time of arrival

Expectants: Casualties who are expected to die

Fast Movers: Jet aircraft.

Field Surgical Kit: Kit carried by medics in the field for small surgery and suturing.

Five by five: Used in radio communications to indicate the radio is working and messages are heard loud and clear.

Flaky: To be in a state of mental disarray or disorganized

Flare, MK-13: A flare that had both a day and night end. The night end generated a very bright light that was visible for a long distance, while the day end gave off a thick cloud of bright orange smoke, see smoke grenade.

Flare, Pen-gun: Illumination projectile; hand-fired

Grids: Maps are broken into numbered thousand-meter squares and each is a grid.

HQ: Headquarters

Huey: Nickname for UH-1 helicopters

Hump: Military term: walk carrying a rucksack in the field.

IG: Inspector General

Immersion foot: Condition resulting from feet being submerged in water or being wet for a prolonged period of time, causing cracking and bleeding. Easily prevented by keeping the feet dry and using clean socks.

Insert: To be deployed into a tactical area, usually by helicopter

K-bar: Combat knife

Klick: Kilometer

Litters: Stretchers to carry wounded

LT: Lieutenant

LZ: Landing zone. Usually a small clearing secured temporarily for the landing of resupply helicopters or Medevac's.

Medevac: Medical evacuation helicopter used in combat areas and in peacetime

Meals Ready to Eat (MRE): Military meals. Small sealed pouches that contains an entrée and side dish, along with a dessert and other small food items. They do not require heating but taste better hot. Lightweight with a high calorie count.

MIA: Missing in action. Meaning lost or missing as a result of combat with an enemy force.

Mike(s): Minute or minutes

NCO: Noncommissioned officer.

Number one: The best of anything

Number ten: The worst or no good.

OD: Olive drab is a color of green used by the military

Forest Penetrator: A device lowered by a winch from a chopper to the ground to pick up survivors. Has a safety strap, seat, and can be used in thick forests or in limited visibility situations.

PJ: (Poppa Juliet) Pararescueman, which used to be called Para-Jumpers. A highly trained individual who works as a rescue specialist and medic. Trained for rescue and recovery.

Point: The forward most man on a military patrol

Poncho liner: Nylon insert to the military rain poncho, used as a blanket frequently.

Pop smoke: To ignite a smoke grenade to signal a rescue aircraft or show wind direction.

PRC-25: Portable Radio Communications, Model 25. A back-packed FM receiver-transmitter used for short-distance communications. The range of the radio was 5-10 kilometers, depending on the weather, unless attached to a special, non-portable antenna which could extend the range to 20-30 kilometers

PRC-90: Small portable hand-held survival radio, usually carried in a survival vest or packed in a survival kit for aircrew members. Range was Generally line of site and very poor in mountainous terrain.

RTO: Radio telephone operator.

Ruck / rucksack: Term used for a backpack issued to military personnel.

Saddle up: Put a pack on and get ready to move out

Slack man: The second man back, from the point, on a military patrol, directly behind the point man, or first man.

Smoke grenade: A grenade that releases brightly colored smoke. Used for signaling Medevac and rescue choppers. Used mostly by other services and not as much by the United States Air Force. Air Force personnel would use a MK-13 smoke signal, with bright orange smoke.

SOP: Standard operating procedure or the written way things are done.

Stokes litter: A basket looking device, similar to a stretcher that is lowered by winch from a chopper to a survivor for pick up.

Starlight scope: A night scope to intensify images at night by using reflected light from the moon, stars or any other source of light.

SRU-21/P Survival Vest: A mesh vest worn by aircrew members that contains survival gear to keep them alive and to assist in rescue. It has flares, radio, matches and much more for survival.

Strobe Light: Hand held strobe light for marking landing zones at night

Team Leader: The leader of a team of military men and he/she is in charge. The team leader can be either an officer or NCO, depending on the mission.

UH-1H: a Huey helicopter

Wood line: A row of trees at the edge of a field

About the Author

**W.R. Benton** is an Amazon Best Selling Author and has previously authored books of fiction, non-fiction and Southern humor. Such notable authors as Matt Braun, Stephen Lodge, Don Bendell, and many others have endorsed his work. His survival book, "*Simple Survival, a Family Outdoors Guide*," is a 2005 Silver Award Winner from the Military Writers Society of American. Additionally, this book was added to the prestigious Estes Park Library in Colorado. James Drury, "The Virginian," endorsed his latest two Western books, "*War Paint*" and "*James McKay, U.S. Army Scout*."

Mister Benton has an Associate Degree in Search and Rescue, Survival Operations, a Baccalaureate in Occupational Safety and Health, and a Masters Degree in Psychology completed except for his thesis. Sergeant Benton retired from the military in 1997, with over twenty-six years of active duty, and at the rank of Senior Master Sergeant (E-8) He spent twelve years as a Life Support Instructor where he taught aircrew members how to use survival gear, survival procedures, and parachuting techniques. Gary has attended the following United States Air Force Survival Schools:

Basic Survival Training
Water Survival Training
Jungle Survival Training
Arctic Survival Training

Sergeant Benton also has over 12 years of classroom instruction as a Life Support Instructor, where he trained thousands of men and women.

Mr. Benton and his wife, Melanie, live near Jackson, Mississippi, with three dogs and two cats.

To learn more about W.R. Benton, visit www.simplesurvival.net or www.wrbenton.net.

Facebook   https://www.facebook.com/wrbenton01